LOVE AND THE CLANS

Now walking along the river bank the Duke wished he had brought his fishing rod with him.

He was certain that if he had done so he would have managed to catch at least one or two fresh young salmon.

Then suddenly he saw just ahead of him that there was someone fishing.

And it was on *his* bank of the river.

He wondered for a moment who it could be.

Perhaps his mother in his absence in London had given permission to a visitor or a tourist to fish there.

Then he was certain that, as he had been back for two days, she would have told him if there had been any such arrangement.

There was no doubt that the person fishing ahead of him was a trespasser and a poacher!

There were bushes on the side of the river and the river itself curved so that the Duke did not have a clear view of the intruder until he had passed through some trees into the open.

It was then he saw that just ahead of him was a *woman*.

And she was fishing in *his* river!

THE BARBARA CARTLAND PINK COLLECTION

Titles in this series

1. The Cross Of Love
2. Love In The Highlands
3. Love Finds The Way
4. The Castle Of Love
5. Love Is Triumphant
6. Stars In The Sky
7. The Ship Of Love
8. A Dangerous Disguise
9. Love Became Theirs
10. Love Drives In
11. Sailing To Love
12. The Star Of Love
13. Music Is The Soul Of Love
14. Love In The East
15. Theirs To Eternity
16. A Paradise On Earth
17. Love Wins In Berlin
18. In Search Of Love
19. Love Rescues Rosanna
20. A Heart In Heaven
21. The House Of Happiness
22. Royalty Defeated By Love
23. The White Witch
24. They Sought Love
25. Love Is The Reason For Living
26. They Found Their Way To Heaven
27. Learning To Love
28. Journey To Happiness
29. A Kiss In The Desert
30. The Heart Of Love
31. The Richness Of Love
32. For Ever And Ever
33. An Unexpected Love
34. Saved By An Angel
35. Touching The Stars
36. Seeking Love
37. Journey To Love
38. The Importance Of Love
39. Love By The Lake
40. A Dream Come True
41. The King Without A Heart
42. The Waters Of Love
43. Danger To The Duke
44. A Perfect Way To Heaven
45. Follow Your Heart
46. In Hiding
47. Rivals For Love
48. A Kiss From The Heart
49. Lovers In London
50. This Way To Heaven
51. A Princess Prays
52. Mine For Ever
53. The Earl's Revenge
54. Love At The Tower
55. Ruled By Love
56. Love Came From Heaven
57. Love And Apollo
58. The Keys Of Love
59. A Castle Of Dreams
60. A Battle Of Brains
61. A Change Of Hearts
62. It Is Love
63. The Triumph Of Love
64. Wanted – A Royal Wife
65. A Kiss Of Love
66. To Heaven With Love
67. Pray For Love
68. The Marquis Is Trapped
69. Hide And Seek For Love
70. Hiding From Love
71. A Teacher Of Love
72. Money Or Love
73. The Revelation Is Love
74. The Tree Of Love
75. The Magnificent Marquis
76. The Castle
77. The Gates Of Paradise
78. A Lucky Star
79. A Heaven On Earth
80. The Healing Hand
81. A Virgin Bride
82. The Trail To Love
83. A Royal Love Match
84. A Steeplechase For Love
85. Love At Last
86. Search For A Wife
87. Secret Love
88. A Miracle Of Love
89. Love And The Clans

LOVE AND THE CLANS

BARBARA CARTLAND

Barbaracartland.com Ltd

ISBN 978-1-908411-51-8

*The characters and situations in this book are entirely
imaginary and bear no relation to any real person or actual
happening.*

Printed and bound in Great Britain by Mimeo
of Huntingdon, Cambridgeshire.

THE BARBARA CARTLAND PINK COLLECTION

Dame Barbara Cartland is still regarded as the most prolific bestselling author in the history of the world.

In her lifetime she was frequently in the Guinness Book of Records for writing more books than any other living author.

Her most amazing literary feat was to double her output from 10 books a year to over 20 books a year when she was 77 to meet the huge demand.

She went on writing continuously at this rate for 20 years and wrote her very last book at the age of 97, thus completing an incredible 400 books between the ages of 77 and 97.

Her publishers finally could not keep up with this phenomenal output, so at her death in 2000 she left behind an amazing 160 unpublished manuscripts, something that no other author has ever achieved.

Barbara's son, Ian McCorquodale, together with his daughter Iona, felt that it was their sacred duty to publish all these titles for Barbara's millions of admirers all over the world who so love her wonderful romances.

So in 2004 they started publishing the 160 brand new Barbara Cartlands as *The Barbara Cartland Pink Collection*, as Barbara's favourite colour was always pink – and yet more pink!

The Barbara Cartland Pink Collection is published monthly exclusively by Barbaracartland.com and the books are numbered in sequence from 1 to 160.

Enjoy receiving a brand new Barbara Cartland book each month by taking out an annual subscription to the Pink Collection, or purchase the books individually.

The Pink Collection is available from the Barbara Cartland website www.barbaracartland.com via mail order and through all good bookshops.

In addition Ian and Iona are proud to announce that The Barbara Cartland Pink Collection is now available in ebook format as from Valentine's Day 2011.

For more information, please contact us at:

Barbaracartland.com Ltd.
Camfield Place
Hatfield
Hertfordshire AL9 6JE
United Kingdom

Telephone: +44 (0)1707 642629
Fax: +44 (0)1707 663041
Email: info@barbaracartland.com

THE LATE DAME BARBARA CARTLAND

Barbara Cartland who sadly died in May 2000 at the age of nearly 99 was the world's most famous romantic novelist who wrote 723 books in her lifetime with worldwide sales of over 1 billion copies and her books were translated into 36 different languages.

As well as romantic novels, she wrote historical biographies, 6 autobiographies, theatrical plays, books of advice on life, love, vitamins and cookery. She also found time to be a political speaker and television and radio personality.

She wrote her first book at the age of 21 and this was called *Jigsaw*. It became an immediate bestseller and sold 100,000 copies in hardback and was translated into 6 different languages. She wrote continuously throughout her life, writing bestsellers for an astonishing 76 years. Her books have always been immensely popular in the United States, where in 1976 her current books were at numbers 1 & 2 in the B. Dalton bestsellers list, a feat never achieved before or since by any author.

Barbara Cartland became a legend in her own lifetime and will be best remembered for her wonderful romantic novels, so loved by her millions of readers throughout the world.

Her books will always be treasured for their moral message, her pure and innocent heroines, her good looking and dashing heroes and above all her belief that the power of love is more important than anything else in everyone's life.

"One of my most favourite quotations on the glorious subject of love comes from an ancient source and is, 'who would choose to forego love so as to spare themselves the agony of loss'."

Barbara Cartland

CHAPTER ONE
1876

"But you *must* marry sooner or later and you *must* marry money."

The Dowager Duchess spoke up with a determined note in her voice that her son recognised only too well.

The Duke of Barenlock walked to the window and looked out at the sea.

"I have already told you, Mama," he said quietly, "that, although the girls in London would have been only too willing to accept me because I am a Duke, they would not fit in here at the Castle."

"I don't know that you mean by that," the Dowager Duchess replied.

"I think you do, Mama. You have always been a wonderful hostess to anyone who is staying here. Also you know, without my saying it, that everyone in the village loves you."

For a moment she could not think of how to reply and then, as she rose from her chair in which she had been sitting with her sewing, she sighed,

"You always have an answer to everything, Alpin, but at twenty-seven it is high time you settled down and produced an heir."

She felt that now she had had the last word and had no wish to prolong the conversation.

She therefore walked out of the library, closing the door behind her.

The Duke turned again to gaze at the sea.

Barenlock Castle was indeed one of the North of Scotland's greatest houses. It had been built in 1400 and the Chieftain of the McBaren Clan had always lived there.

The Duke owned thousands of acres in the County of Sutherland and the Castle was undoubtedly one of the most beautiful buildings ever erected in Scotland.

The only difficulty there had been down the ages was to make sure that there was an heir to the Dukedom that came from a very ancient lineage.

As the present Duke was an only child, his mother and all his relations continually begged him, almost on their knees, to take a wife.

The Duke travelled a great deal and spent a certain amount of time every year in London and as he was tall, handsome and most intelligent, it was not surprising that ambitious mothers presented their daughters to him.

Yet, for some reason his family could not discover, he always returned from London alone, still a bachelor and apparently with his heart untroubled.

"What you have to realise," his mother had said to him over and over again, "is that as Head of the family and of the Clan, it is your duty to marry and produce an heir – several sons if possible. You must carry on the traditions we have all followed even before the Castle was built."

The Duke had heard this lecture so often he knew every sentence by heart.

But he listened to his mother because he loved her and he knew that she adored him.

He had heard the same plea over and over again and it merely made him more determined than ever.

He would not marry until he found someone he loved and with whom he would know intuitively that he would be happy and content.

Of course there were women in his life and a great number of them.

His many and frequent *affaires-de-coeur* had been well known in London and whispered about amongst the Clan in Scotland.

On his last visit, from which he had just returned, his name had been linked with one of the most beautiful and sensual ladies in Mayfair.

She was in fact herself a Baroness and half English and half French.

She was incredibly lovely and her husband closed his eyes to her indiscretions.

As he said to one of his friends confidentially,

"I am growing too old to be fighting a duel at dawn every other day. So I just close my eyes, shut my ears and when my wife returns to me, as she always does, I think not of the past but of the future."

This strange *laissez-faire* attitude enabled the Duke to spend a very pleasant two months making love to the glamorous Baroness. He was entranced by her as all her lovers were.

Not only was it her alluring beauty that excited him but the subtle way she invariably made him feel he was the only man in her life at that very moment.

Now that he was back in Scotland the Duke was having to listen to the usual family refrain that he should be married – if he did not do so, how would the McBarens survive without a Chieftain?

"They survived under another Chieftain before I was born," he had muttered yesterday to his mother, "and I imagine they will survive after I am dead."

"I cannot think how you can talk like that, Alpin. You know how much our name means in Scotland and if you married a rich wife, we could do all the repairs to the Castle we have been dying to undertake for so long now."

The Duke made a sound, but did not interrupt her.

"And, of course," she rattled on, "you could build the museum you have contributed so much to and make it one of the most celebrated in the whole of Scotland."

The Duke knew this to be true.

Unfortunately, as he had so often pointed out, their name explained the difficulty they were now in.

When the Vikings first came to Scotland, one of the easiest places for them to land was at the bay where the Castle now stood.

There had been an old and dilapidated keep on the site now occupied by the Castle that possessed, so legend related, many treasures that had been stolen by violence from other Clans and this plunder had made the owners of the Castle exceedingly rich.

It had always been a great tragedy for the family when later the Vikings had taken away everything they could pack into their ships, as well as the most attractive young maidens in the neighbourhood.

That they had stolen the Clan's cattle was of course a familiar story.

But the Duke, even when he was a small boy, had always regretted that he had not seen the treasure that had been taken from the old keep, even though it had been acquired quite illegally by his Clan in the first place.

It was when the old keep was finally demolished that the Clan had changed its name to McBaren.

They claimed that they now possessed nothing and they had no wish to remember the happier days when they had been so powerful.

4

Then their fortunes changed.

The Chief of the Clan had married a great heiress from the North of England.

It was she who had built the new Castle and it was she who had made the Clan, despite the fact they had kept the name of McBaren, more powerful than any other Clan in the North.

The Castle had then been added to year after year and the Dukedom, an English title, was presented to the McBarens at the end of the seventeenth century.

Money had been spent on the estate in a manner that had made the rest of Scotland gasp.

It was not only the Castle itself that grew larger and more beautiful year by year, but there were villages with delightful houses built round it.

There were gardens filled with flowers that seemed to have come from Fairyland and were attended by a whole army of gardeners.

But it was only when the Fourth Duke became the Chieftain of the Clan that it was discovered that his father had been spending enormously above his income – in fact the whole estate was steadily moving into debt.

"I just cannot believe it," the Dowager Duchess had moaned a thousand times.

But unfortunately it was too true.

It was therefore quite obvious that since the Clan was dependent on him, the Duke must put matters to right.

As he was so good-looking, he could easily marry an heiress and she would make the Clan as powerful as it had been in the past.

The only difficulty was the Duke himself.

"I will not," he had insisted over and over again, "be pushed into marrying someone simply because she is rich.

I cannot imagine anything more hateful than being bound to a woman I do not love, and who could then make life exceedingly unpleasant for me if she holds onto the purse strings."

"But, dearest, we just cannot go on as we are," his mother would retort. "We are overdrawn at the bank and there are thousands of repairs and renewals that require urgent attention on the estate."

The Duke did not question her and she continued,

"One of our tenant farmers who lives on the border of the estate called in to see you yesterday. As you were out, he told me a really pitiful story of how the MacFallins are stealing our cattle and making life impossible for those who are trying to keep their heads above water in that part of the County."

The Duke sighed deeply.

For the last three centuries the McBarens had been the enemies of the MacFallins.

This animosity between the Clans had broken out from time to time into actual fighting.

Now they were merely stealing each other's sheep and cattle or, if they met in a village pub, fought each other verbally and sometimes with their fists.

All for no particular reason except that each hated the other Clan.

Now that his mother had left the room, the Duke tried to forget all they had been talking about.

Instead he wanted to appreciate the beauty of the flowers beneath him and, beyond the immaculately tended garden, there was the shining sea.

It always pleased the Duke when he returned from the South that he could travel home in his yacht rather than by train.

Then he could sail into the bay below the Castle and walk from the wooden jetty into his own garden.

It was at such times that he told himself how lucky he was.

Yet he knew as soon as he arrived that there would be a certain look in his mother's eyes and it signalled a repeated question to which he alone held the answer.

'I cannot do it,' he would mutter to himself when he walked up to bed after a long argument.

Now, as he always felt upset when they quarrelled, he walked out into the garden and down to the sea.

It was a glorious day with the sun shining through a clear sky.

The waves seemed to be dancing with a light that came from the Heavens.

The Duke stood for a long time gazing dreamily out to sea.

He wished that he was in a ship setting forth on an adventure to foreign lands –

*

When finally he returned to the Castle, it was to find his mother waiting for him.

With her was one of his relations who lived about five miles away. It was Moira, the Countess of Dunkeld.

"I heard you were back, Alpin," she began, "and I am sure you enjoyed yourself in London."

"I did, Cousin Moira," he replied, "and it was very gratifying to be invited so often to Marlborough House."

"Oh, do tell us what that naughty Prince of Wales is doing now," his cousin begged.

She and her husband owned a house and a small estate that had been in the hands of the Dunkeld family for almost as long as the Dukes had been at Castle Barenlock.

"Of course," the Countess carried on, "we were all hoping you would bring back exciting news that you were to be married. But your mother tells me no lovely lady in the *Beau Monde* has yet touched your heart and you are still determined to remain a bachelor."

"I will not be forced into marriage, which is a very different thing," the Duke replied somewhat aggressively.

"Well, I have news for you," the Countess added. "I have two charming girls coming to stay with me. One is my daughter, Charlotte, who you know and the other is a very rich – very attractive American!"

She said the last words slowly, emphasising them.

The Duke laughed.

"If you are trying to tempt me up the aisle with an American, you are wasting your time. There were quite a number of them in London, all very keen to return home with a title. In fact I believe a few Italians have availed themselves already of such pleasant offers."

"But you refused even to contemplate them. Oh, dearest Alpin, what can we do with you?"

"The answer to that is quite simple, Cousin Moira, I want to be left alone. When I do find the right person I wish to marry, I will naturally notify you all."

He stalked out of the room as he finished speaking.

His mother looked towards the Countess and made a helpless gesture with her hands.

"It's no use, Moira, I have talked and talked again to Alpin, but he is so determined not to marry and, as you well know, it is vital that he does in order to save the Castle and the estate."

"I am sorry for you," the Countess murmured. "I think it is infuriating of Alpin not to be more responsible.

"He must surely be well aware that everything is becoming more and more dilapidated. The Clansmen are growing restless at not being able to buy new stock at the sheep markets and the rivers are not looked after as they should be."

"I hear that the poaching is terrible," the Dowager Duchess added.

"I am afraid it's true. Night after night, we are told, poachers move up the river. Neither of us employ enough river watchers to prevent them taking away large hauls of our salmon."

The Dowager Duchess sighed.

"I have told Alpin about it over and over again, but he still says he will not marry until he actually wants to."

There was silence before she added quickly,

"What is the American girl like you are bringing here tomorrow?"

"She is very attractive and I think quite intelligent. Her father is enormously rich. I believe that he has struck oil amongst other things and also has made a great deal of money from the new steamships America is now building."

"While we just sit here and watch the bricks falling off the top of the Castle," said the Dowager Duchess, "and the land remains uncultivated because we cannot afford the wages of any more men to work on it."

"You must not be depressed, dearest," the Countess replied. "I am sure that sooner or later Alpin will see sense and come home with a bride we can all welcome with open arms."

"He is far more likely to present us with some girl of his own choice who does not have a penny to her name!"

"I will talk to him again tonight, Moira. I know he loves me and does want to make me happy. I feel if this American girl is really so rich, he must understand that he has to sacrifice himself for the good of the Clan."

"I hope you will be able to make him realise that it all rests in his hands. We cannot do more than offer him peaches on a plate and only hope he will pick one up!"

The Countess glanced at the clock and rose.

"I must return to my home," she said. "My guests are arriving some time after tea and I will bring them over tomorrow for sure."

"I think that it would be a good idea," the Dowager Duchess suggested, "if they stayed here. Why not say you are shorthanded or that the roof of the kitchen has fallen in and therefore you are all coming to stay to the Castle?"

"That's an excellent idea. Actually it is what I would prefer anyway because two of our bedrooms have to be redecorated and the girls are each bringing their lady's maid with them."

She paused before she added,

"Of course they are coming up from London with a chaperone, but she unfortunately is going back tomorrow morning."

"Well, I will look forward to seeing you all before luncheon, Moira. I am sure that your American girl will be entranced by the Castle and of course by Alpin too."

The Countess gave a laugh.

"He is so handsome and I have been told there were a dozen girls in London only too willing to rush into his arms if he even raised his little finger!"

The Dowager Duchess sighed.

"How can he be so stupid? There must have been at least one young girl who I would gladly have welcomed here as my daughter-in-law."

"Of course there were, Eleanor. And as Alpin is so friendly with the Prince of Wales, he has undoubtedly met all the greatest beauties and all the greatest heiresses."

"As I have pointed out to him often enough, Moira, he is getting older."

The Countess giggled.

"We are all doing that, but you, dearest Eleanor, were always a beauty and the story of how your husband fell in love with you the first moment he saw you has been handed down to us all."

The Dowager Duchess smiled.

She had been just sixteen at the time and had come back unexpectedly early from school because an epidemic had been threatening the younger girls and holidays had therefore started earlier than expected.

The Duke of Barenlock was staying for the night with her father and mother. He was a widower of thirty-two, his wife having died having their first child, who had not survived either.

A young schoolgirl came running excitedly into the drawing room so that she could fling her arms around her father and mother.

The Duke took one glance at her and fell in love.

He was obliged to wait until she was a year older and then they were married and were exceedingly happy until the Duke died.

Their only disappointment was they only had one child, but, as he was a son to carry on the Dukedom, it was not such a tragedy as it might have been.

There were a good number of men who would have loved to make the widowed Duchess their wife, but she had been so deeply in love with her husband that she found it impossible to contemplate marriage with anyone else.

It was indeed a very romantic story.

The Countess could not understand why Alpin did not make his mother happy by taking a wife and bringing, as they hoped, both plenty of money and several children into the Castle.

However she kissed the Dowager Duchess goodbye and said,

"I will see you tomorrow before luncheon. If you are sensible you will not talk too much about the American heiress until Alpin sees her. I am certain that he will then find it impossible not to marry her."

"I only hope you are right, Moira, but you know what Alpin is like. If he has made up his mind, he will not marry an American or any other foreigner for that matter, then nothing I can say or do will change him."

"Just keep your fingers crossed and believe there is always another time."

She kissed the Dowager Duchess again and then hurried downstairs where her carriage was waiting outside the front door.

As she drove off, she looked up at the towers of the Castle.

She thought that any girl, especially one from the other side of the Atlantic, would be entranced by anything so stunningly beautiful – so obviously like a fairy story.

*

The Duke was certain that the Countess would be talking about him to his mother and so he therefore decided to walk up the river that ran into the sea just North of the Castle.

He had arranged to go fishing tomorrow morning and he had not gone out after breakfast today as he usually did because he wanted to be with his mother,

He was well aware that he had disappointed her by coming back from London 'empty-handed' as it were.

But he had spent all of his time with the beautiful Baroness and had therefore not paid any attention to the *debutantes* who were invariably paraded in front of him at every party he attended.

The only exception of course was at Marlborough House where *all* the ladies were married and the men, like himself, were young and unattached and devoted admirers of the many beauties who surrounded the Prince of Wales.

There was, needless to say, not an unmarried girl amongst them and the Duke enjoyed many sophisticated flirtations with entrancing and witty ladies.

'Why,' he asked himself as he walked along the bank of the river, 'should I give up that for some tiresome young girl without a single brain in her head, who would doubtless bore me to death a week after I had placed the ring on her finger?'

The few *debutantes* he had already met in London he had found definitely unattractive – they giggled at what he had to say and blushed if he paid them a compliment.

He was speaking truthfully when he told his mother that he would be bored stiff with any one of them almost before they had left the Church!

He was determined to explore a great deal more of the world before he finally settled down and produced the much-wanted heir.

In the meantime, as far as he was concerned, the Castle would have to wait to be repaired and the Clansmen must look after themselves.

He did, however, grudge the fact that the poachers were spoiling his own sport on the river – they were having a free hand at night to take away as many salmon as they pleased.

"What we need, Your Grace," his ghillie had said as soon as he went fishing, "be at least two or three more river watchers, then yon devils'll not sneak in somehow and take the salmon afore we can stop 'em."

The Duke knew that he was not exaggerating.

He enjoyed fishing almost as much as he enjoyed shooting and so he resented that his special river, like other rivers on his estate, was being pilfered almost every night.

He had at the moment no wish to go back to the Castle and listen to the Countess lecturing him endlessly on the attractiveness of some American heiress.

So he walked further up the river than he intended – to almost the end of his estate in that part of the County.

It had always been a bitter knowledge to the Dukes of Barenlock that one part of their estate which had once been theirs was now held by their rival Clan, the dreaded MacFallins, who had settled there two centuries ago.

Because the McBaren Clan at the time had not the strength to remove them, they had been there ever since and they had systematically extended their land claims.

The Duke was a big landowner, but the great part of his land lay South of the Castle and extended West almost to the other side of Scotland.

The land belonging to the MacFallins was nothing like as extensive as his.

Yet a bitter rivalry had sprung up over the centuries between the two Clans and like many others in Scotland they hated each other so heartily that when they were not actually fighting, they expressed their mutual animosity in language that in polite Society was unrepeatable.

What annoyed the Duke more than anything else was that this particular river, which was his favourite, ran directly through the MacFallin estate and as usual there was continued rivalry as to who caught the most salmon.

The part of the river belonging to the MacFallins ran for about a mile through moorland and then it widened into a large loch under some high hills.

It was the loch which the Duke would have liked to own, although he owned a great many other lochs to the South and the excellent salmon rivers connected to them.

Yet automatically he was irritated that part of his special river ran through MacFallin territory.

He had often thought that it really was ridiculous for the two Clans to hate each other as they undoubtedly did.

The MacFallins were too prudent to venture except rarely onto land belonging to the McBarens and the same applied to the Duke's men who seldom encroached on land claimed by the MacFallins.

'The whole situation is ridiculous,' the Duke often thought, 'we should have grown out of this nonsense years ago.'

But unfortunately the mutual hatred was still there.

Whenever the Earl MacFallin, who reigned over the MacFallin Clan met the Duke at the County games or any other official occasion, they only nodded to each other and never spoke a word.

Occasionally the Duke received furious letters from the Earl claiming that his land had been trespassed on or that a McBaren had stolen some of his sheep.

The Duke never responded by answering the letters himself. Instead he ordered one of his staff to do so and he learnt that the Earl was extremely offensive about him.

Now walking along the river bank the Duke wished he had brought his fishing rod with him.

He was certain that if he had done so he would have managed to catch at least one or two fresh young salmon.

Then suddenly he saw just ahead of him that there was someone fishing.

And it was on *his* bank of the river.

He wondered for a moment who it could be.

Perhaps his mother in his absence in London had given permission to a visitor or a tourist to fish there.

Then he was certain that, as he had been back for two days, she would have told him if there had been any such arrangement.

There was no doubt that the person fishing ahead of him was a trespasser and a poacher!

There were bushes on the side of the river and the river itself curved so that the Duke did not have a clear view of the intruder until he had passed through some trees into the open.

It was then he saw that just ahead of him was a *woman*.

And she was fishing in *his* river!

She was definitely a stranger on his land.

So he walked towards her quickly and angrily.

"What on earth are you doing here?" he barked at her sharply while she still had her back to him.

She gave a little cry and turned round.

He could now see that she was quite young and not unattractive.

"I am – sorry," she stammered. "Have I come – too far? I was told to stop where the MacFallin land ended, but I did not know – exactly where that was."

"You are on *my* ground," the Duke said sternly, "and you are in fact poaching. So I would be grateful if you would go back up the river for at least a quarter of a mile."

"Yes, of course, and I am sorry – so very sorry," the woman muttered.

She started to reel in her line.

Then she gave a sudden cry.

"It's a salmon! What do you want me to do?"

The Duke had intended to tell her to shake it off as it was his salmon and yet she was fishing extremely well.

Keeping a tight line on the salmon, at the same time dropping the tip of the rod whenever it leapt.

She was so excited at the prospect of a catch, he felt he could not give her an order to shake it off.

The fish was fighting hard for its freedom and the Duke appreciated that this woman knew exactly what she was doing.

She was keeping her fish tightly under control with an expertise he night have shown himself.

She had by now moved a little further down the river and yet she still had complete control of the salmon which was fresh and must have just come into the river from the sea.

Almost without thinking about it the Duke picked up her net which was lying on the ground and followed her down the riverbank.

Finally, after an enthralling battle, the salmon could fight no longer and she began to wind in her line.

The fish made a last desperate effort to escape, but the Duke bent forward and caught it in the net.

"I have done it at last! I have really done it!" the girl exclaimed. "I knew I would catch a salmon if I was lucky, but I would never have landed it if you had not been here to lift it out of the water for me."

She was speaking so excitedly that the Duke asked,

"Is this the first salmon you have ever caught?"

"My very first salmon!" she replied. "I have caught trout at home on our river, but this is different. It's the most exciting thing I have ever done."

The Duke smiled.

He remembered he had felt like that when he had caught *his* first salmon.

Then he had been a boy of only eight years old and he had taken it home proudly to show it to his father and mother – they had been delighted because it was almost as big as he was.

He bent down to take the hook from the salmon's mouth, saying as he did so,

"This is a fresh fish which has just come in from the sea. I think you should have it stuffed and keep it as a memento of your first salmon."

The young woman laughed.

"I didn't expect that anyone would admire it except myself," she said. "My father has caught so many he is quite blasé about it."

She looked down at the salmon and then she added,

"I suppose if I behave properly – I should give it to you as I caught it in your water."

"Let me make you a present of it," said the Duke generously. "It would be very cruel to deprive you of your first salmon whether you eat it or keep it."

The girl was kneeling down looking at her catch as if she could hardly believe she had been clever enough to make it hers.

It was about six pounds in weight.

Then the Duke asked her,

"Have you far to carry it or would you like me to help you?"

The girl looked up at him and he saw that her eyes were very blue against her pink and white skin.

"It is very kind of you to suggest it," she replied. "Actually I came down to the river with a ghillie. But he cut his hand rather badly on some glass which had been left lying about and went off to have it bound up and told me to continue fishing down the river."

"He, of course, would have told you exactly where the boundary was – "

The girl looked round and then she remarked,

"I suppose I am on the land of the McBarens who we have always hated, but I often thought perhaps they are not as bad as we think they are."

The Duke stared at her and then he said slowly,

"From the way you speak I should imagine that *you* are a MacFallin."

"Yes I am," the girl replied and then she gave a sudden cry,

"You are not the Duke of Barenlock? You cannot be!"

"Is that such a terrible thing?" the Duke asked with a smile.

"I never imagined – I didn't think the Duke would look as you do, Your Grace."

"I'm sorry if I disappoint you."

"Of course you don't," she answered. "I always thought of the Duke as being old and ugly and looking somehow like the devil!"

The Duke laughed.

"It's so silly of me to think like that," she went on. "But ever since I can remember my father and my uncles have been saying horrible things about you. Why should they do that?"

"You must be well aware that the Scottish Clans are always fighting someone. There is not at the moment any enemy from abroad or from England, so they fight amongst themselves!"

"Yes, of course, I have known that, Your Grace, but now I am home it seems rather ridiculous."

"Where have you been?" the Duke enquired.

"I was brought up by my grandmother because she was lonely. As we are quite a large family, I was sent to live with her in London."

"So you know little about Scotland?"

"Very little," she answered. "I have not been here for five years. Then I only stayed for a short time."

"Why are you here now?" the Duke questioned her.

"Because my grandmother has died and I have now come home to my family in Scotland."

She gave a little sigh.

"It is rather hard adjusting to them after not seeing them for so long. When they jeered at me for not having caught a salmon, I went out to see what I could do about it!"

"And you have been very successful."

He stood up leaving the fish still in the net.

"I think what I had better do," he suggested, "is to carry your fish for you back to the road. There is sure to be someone on it going in the direction of your father's house and you will easily find a lift."

"That is very kind of you," the girl replied, "but I feel guilty, after having poached your salmon, to let you carry it. It is almost insulting."

The Duke laughed.

"I daresay I will survive, even though our ancestors have been at each others' throats for generations!"

"Yes, and I do think it's very stupid of them."

"Tell me your name," the Duke asked her.

"It's Sheinna. It is Gaelic for 'singing'."

"And do you sing?"

"I do as a matter of fact. Actually it has even been suggested I should go on the stage. But my grandmother was horrified at the idea and I feel that my father would be too."

"What are you going to do now you have returned home?" the Duke asked her.

"I am going to learn to fish and I suppose be told how terrible you and your Clan are. I remember they were hurling endless insults about you McBarens almost before I could talk!"

"It seems ridiculous in this day and age we should carry on fighting each other, Sheinna. There are far more important people to fight."

"Like all those poachers, Your Grace. My father is furious about what they have done on the other side of his land and I am told that this side is also infested at night. Of course he blames you for not keeping a closer watch on your rivers."

"I wish I could do so, but unfortunately, like a great number of others, I just cannot afford to employ as many men as I would like to do, especially when it concerns river watchers."

"Are you hard-up?" Sheinna enquired. "I always believed you to be enormously rich and sitting counting out your gold pounds, while we always had to think hard before we spent them!"

"I do wish my gold pounds were true, but they only exist in my imagination – "

"And of course in the stories," added Sheinna, "of the great treasures that were stolen from you many years ago by the Vikings."

The Duke chuckled.

"So you know that story."

"Of course I do. My Nanny used to tell me all the stories of Scotland, especially this part of the Highlands. I must say I not only love every one of them but remember them all."

"I am sure there are a great number of them I have not heard," said the Duke. "Perhaps it would be an idea if I asked you to write some of them down for me or else tell them to me when we next meet. In return I will give you permission to fish tomorrow on the same piece of water you fished over today."

"Would you really do that, Your Grace?" Sheinna asked.

Then she looked away from him and he knew her expression was troubled.

"You think that your father would disapprove," he quizzed her.

"Yes, of course, that is just what I was thinking. He hates your Clan, as we were all brought up to hate you. I suppose you and I can do nothing about it."

"I tell you what we will do. Just because it annoys me that this animosity should continue between our two Clans, if you get up early tomorrow morning, Sheinna, and come down here alone, I will meet you and act as your ghillie."

The girl's eyes twinkled.

"Think how angry Papa will be, and so will your Clan, if they get to know about it."

"I think they are unlikely to do so. As you have been so successful with my salmon, I really think I must help you to catch two or three more before we return to throwing mud at each other!"

Sheinna laughed and it was a very pretty sound.

"I will never do that after you have been so kind, Your Grace. You could have made me shake it off and then all my life I would sigh for the fish I never caught."

"Now you will be able to dream about the one you have caught and I think it is only fair that you should catch two or three more."

"If you are willing to risk it then I would love to do so," answered Sheinna. "But you know what will be said about us if we are seen?"

"I think it will start our Clans fighting as they have never fought before, but we will risk it and, if they do get really nasty, I will just have to ask you to hand me back my salmon, so that I can put it in a glass case and say that I took it from the MacFallins after they had attempted to steal it from me!"

Sheinna giggled.

"That is exactly how a new war may start between us, but that is something you and I must definitely stop if we can."

"We can at least try," the Duke sighed, "and I am sure you will agree with me that the whole animosity is completely ridiculous in the first place. It should certainly be repudiated now we are older and wiser."

He thought as he spoke that the MacFallins were certainly not very much wiser – with the exception of this gloriously pretty girl.

They were now nearing the road.

He could see in the distance that there was a cart being driven slowly towards them.

"I have no idea," he said, "whether it is one of your people or one of mine. But it would be a mistake, if we are to meet tomorrow morning, for whoever is driving it to see us. Goodbye, Lady Sheinna, and I really hope you will be able to slip out at seven o'clock and I will be waiting for you."

"You can be quite certain I will be there," Sheinna replied, "and thank you for being so kind."

She took the fish from the Duke and then walked resolutely towards the road.

He slipped away amongst the trees.

As he reached the river bank and looked back, he could see the cart had turned round and was taking her back the way it had come.

He thought smilingly that it was a very unexpected encounter.

He would certainly try himself tomorrow morning to catch two or three salmon in this river as they were obviously taking.

And it would also be amusing to think how angry Lady Sheinna's father would be if he knew what they were doing together.

CHAPTER TWO

The Duke arrived back at the Castle rather pleased with his morning's work to find that the factor and other workers on his estate were waiting to speak to him.

They gave him encouraging reports on the grouse hatching and the health of his lambs.

"This year, Your Grace," the Head Shepherd said, "we should get a better price at the sales than we've ever had afore."

"That is extremely good news," the Duke told him.

He praised both him and all the men working under him.

He took luncheon with his mother who brought him up-to-date with the latest gossip in the area.

She also informed him that the Countess with the two girls she wanted him to meet were arriving at teatime.

"I did hope to be alone with you, Mama, after being away so long," the Duke muttered.

"I know, my dearest boy, but Moira Dunkeld was determined to bring this American girl to see you and I am sure you will find her charming."

The Duke was certain he would not, but thought it a mistake to argue too much and so he suggested,

"Please try, Mama, to accept me as I am and not try to alter me. You know I am very happy here with you and have no wish at all to have another woman take over the Castle."

His mother sighed, but did not feel like pressing the point at this stage.

Instead she asked him,

"When are you going fishing, my dear?"

"This afternoon, Mama. So if I am late for tea you must make my excuses, but I think it's high time I caught a salmon."

"I know the ghillies are waiting anxiously for you, and they will be most disappointed if you don't make a big catch."

The Duke smiled.

He thought as he walked downstairs, knowing that the ghillies would be ready for him, that fish or no fish he would be late for tea.

As it so happened the salmon were taking well and he caught three beautiful silvery springers.

He was indeed late, but he returned triumphant to the Castle.

His mother was waiting for him in the drawing room.

As soon as he entered, the Duke was aware that a number of eyes were turned in his direction.

He bent to kiss his mother, then held out his hand to the Countess.

"It's so delightful to be back again at the Castle, Cousin Moira," he intoned.

"You have neglected us for too long, Alpin," the Countess replied, "for the festivities you enjoy in London. I am sure that is the right word for them."

"They were certainly most enjoyable, but I am still extremely glad to be home."

"Now I want you to meet two very pretty girls," the Countess continued. "Of course you remember my little daughter Charlotte, although she was only sixteen, I think, when you last saw her."

The Duke shook hands formally with his relation.

Charlotte had certainly changed from the gawky little teenager he remembered into an elegant and pretty *debutante*.

"I am so thrilled to here again in the Castle," she cooed to the Duke. "When I told the girls at my Finishing School that I often came here, they were filled with envy. In fact they all want to visit your Castle."

"I am sure there are plenty of castles for them to see in England," the Duke replied, "without coming so far North."

"Well, Mary-Lee says that there are no castles in America at all and she is thrilled to meet what she calls, 'a real Dook' and to see his Castle!"

The Duke laughed.

He turned and shook hands with a most attractive American-looking girl.

It was extraordinary what a difference there was between her and Charlotte, but he was aware that although they were the same age she looked rather more experienced in many ways than her school friend.

"I think this Castle is real fine," Mary-Lee sighed speaking with an unmistakable American accent. "I want to explore it all from top to bottom."

"You will certainly be allowed to do so," the Duke responded. "And I am sure that Charlotte has not forgotten her way around all the turrets and corridors."

"I know just what Mary-Lee would really like," the Countess interrupted, "and that is that she should be shown round the Castle by its owner."

The Duke reckoned as usual that his relation was trying to insinuate a future bride upon him, but he merely remarked,

27

"If Charlotte has forgotten the way, I know that Rory is a better guide than anyone else."

Rory was the butler who had served his family for many years.

The Duke saw the instant expression of annoyance on his cousin's face when she realised that he was not as easily trapped as she had been hoping.

He sat down near the teatable and as his mother poured him out a cup of tea, he helped himself to a scone.

"Were the fish you caught today big ones, Cousin Alpin," asked Charlotte.

"One was nearly eleven pounds," he answered, "but the other two, I regret to say, were rather smaller."

"Nevertheless you caught them and that is just what I too am longing to do now I have come home. So please can Mary-Lee and I come and fish with you tomorrow?"

"What is happening on your own river?" the Duke asked looking at the Countess.

"We have not been particularly successful so far this season," she replied. "But, as you already know, your river here is better than anyone else's."

"I do like to find out what is happening on the other rivers, Cousin Moira. In fact my own rivers have not been as good as they used to be, so I have been informed,"

"The ghillies alway say that the fishing was better in the past," the Dowager Duchess added. "I have heard that story every year since I first came here. Invariably we always used to do better than any other river in Scotland."

"I expect yours is better protected than ours is," the Countess said. "We know for a fact we are being poached every night. As the poachers keep constantly on the move and we have only two rather ancient river watchers, they never seem to catch them actually at work."

"If you ask me, Moira, I think a great number of poachers are hand in glove with the river watchers. They get a rake-off and therefore shut their eyes to the poaching when it is actually taking place."

"I wonder if that is true," the Duke came in. "I did not think of it before, but it could easily happen."

"It certainly happens up here," the Countess cried. "In fact all the way to Caithness I hear people complaining that nothing seems to be done about it."

"Well, I will certainly give it my full attention now I am home," the Duke promised.

"And *please*, before the poachers take all the fish away, can we come here to see what we can catch in your river?" Charlotte persisted.

"Of course you can," the Duke agreed, "and I will arrange for you to have the very best ghillie to show you where you can fish."

"Thank you, thank you," Charlotte cried. "If Mary-Lee catches a salmon, she is going to have it stuffed and sent back to her father in America to show him that she is a sportswoman, as he never thought her to be!"

"I know my Papa will be very impressed if I catch a fish on a Duke's river," Mary-Lee simpered.

"You will certainly have the opportunity," the Duke added.

"And of course," the Countess asserted, "it would be even more exciting if you, Alpin, were to teach Mary-Lee how to fish as well as you do."

The Duke reflected that once again his cousin was pushing the girl into his arms two minutes after they had been introduced.

He did not answer her and instead he held out his teacup to his mother, saying,

"Can I have some more tea, Mama, and do tell me what you have been doing today."

"Nothing that you would not find extremely boring, my dear, but we do have some amusing people coming to dinner tonight. There will be some young men for the girls as well as a very charming lady who is longing to see you again."

"Who is that?" the Duke enquired suspiciously.

"It is to be a surprise, Alpin. I hope, when you do see her, you will not have forgotten her."

"Tell me who it is," the Duke insisted.

"I will tell you later, my dear."

He thought that once again they were making it clear that he must be amused now he was at home and it seemed impossible for them to realise that he might prefer being alone with his mother.

He wanted to concentrate on his fishing rather than to entertain friends in the neighbourhood and he had never thought that any of them were particularly likable.

He disliked having unfledged young women thrust upon him, but he could see that Mary-Lee was certainly an attractive girl, but he felt certain that she was far too young for him to find he had anything in common with her.

'Except of course,' a voice inside him murmured almost as if it was speaking into his ear, '*she is very rich.*'

He was well aware that was the reason the Countess had brought her over the moment she arrived and he was quite certain she had talked it over with his mother before he came home.

It was obvious to him that they had both decided that he must take a rich wife and the sooner the better.

*

The Duke retired to his study which was also his very special library.

There was another library in the Castle where the family collection of the ancient books of Scotland had been increased by generation after generation.

But in his own study he kept the most up-to-date and modern books.

He had them sent to him from Edinburgh as soon as they were published and it was a special extravagance that he would not give up however difficult the money situation might become.

If he was not actually travelling, he could travel in his mind and he found that books which had recently been published about the Far East particularly appealed to him.

When he closed his study door and sat down at his desk, he thought to himself that the next time he went away he would go further abroad than he had ever been before.

'Otherwise,' he mused, 'I will find myself married sooner rather than later and then it will be impossible for me ever to explore the places I really want to see.'

He longed to visit Nepal and, if possible, although he had been told over and over again it was somewhere he could never reach, he would love to go to Tibet.

'If I wait much longer,' he reflected, 'it will be too late. Undoubtedly I will be trapped into marriage, however much I try to safeguard myself against it.'

He had not been in his study long before the door opened and the Countess peeped in.

"I thought you might be here, Alpin," she blurted out, "and I do want to talk to you."

The Duke rose politely to his feet.

He so wanted to be quiet and alone, but he could hardly be rude to his cousin.

He knew, despite the fact she was always worrying him to get married, that she was extremely fond of him.

"I really have some letters to write, Cousin Moira," he said, "but of course I am delighted to see you again and it is so kind of you to spend so much time with my Mama. I am always afraid that when I am away she will be lonely and unhappy."

"She loves having you at home," said the Countess. "At the same time when you do go away, it is a pity you cannot leave her grandchildren with her."

The Duke held up his hands.

"Not that argument again!" he complained. "You know as well as I do there is plenty of time for me to have a hoard of tiresome children and I have no intention of marrying at the moment."

He spoke firmly as if to impress on his cousin once and for all that her matchmaking was doomed to failure.

However, she merely laughed out loud and then sat down in a comfortable chair.

"Now listen to me, Alpin – "

"Not if it is about marriage. That is a forbidden subject!"

"Forbidden or not, Alpin, I have to inform you that Mary-Lee is one of the richest girls in America. As you know that is very different from saying she is one of the richest girls in England."

"I am *not* interested, Cousin Moira. I can see she is a pretty girl, but I feel almost old enough to be her father. Besides I have no intention at present of marrying anyone."

"Oh really, Alpin, must you be so difficult and so stupid about it?" the Countess reprimanded him.

The Duke did not answer and after a moment she added,

"You would be far happier with a young girl whom you could teach to love you as you want to be loved and who would listen adoringly to everything you said to her, than if you married some stuck-up young woman who is only too aware of her own attractions, especially when the chief amongst them is her moneybags."

"That may be your idea of a happy marriage, but it is not mine. Incidentally, Cousin Moira, I am sick to death of the whole subject and absolutely refuse to discuss it any further."

"It is all very well for you to talk like that. Have you realised that your Castle is falling down for want of repair, that the McBaren estate is sneered at by most of the other Scottish owners in the vicinity and how you yourself are deliberately soiling your proud family name by not doing your duty as one of the most important landowners in the whole of Scotland.

"We all love you and want you to be happy, but, Alpin, you must realise that things cannot go on as they are at the moment."

"I really see nothing wrong with them," the Duke retorted rather truculently. "We are not short of staff and I have not dismissed anyone who was here in my father's time."

"You have not dismissed them, but they have either died or been too old to work for you. You know as well as I do that you are short of shepherds and your river watchers have dwindled until just about every river you possess is a happy hunting ground to the dreaded poachers. As I have said already, the Castle needs a hundred repaints to which you turn a blind eye."

The Duke rose and slowly walked across the room to the window.

He stood looking out at the sea, thinking how fond he was of this particular view and how much the Castle meant to him.

Yet how could he face himself if he married some girl entirely for her money?

She would violate all the dreams he had secretly cherished throughout his life.

And what was more – his own pride.

It was impossible to explain to anyone, even his mother, that he had always believed that one day he would find someone whom he not only loved passionately, but respected and admired.

He would let her rule with him the Kingdom which had been handed down to him over five hundred years.

Everything had seemed to him a sacred trust ever since he was a small boy, when he had thought everything at home in Scotland was perfect and would never change with the years.

Naturally he fully recognised that he needed money and a great deal of it.

Money would pay for very many innovations and endless improvements could be introduced on the estate as on the richer estates in the Lowlands and in England.

But somehow in the far North of Scotland it did not seem to matter so much, except when his contentment was intruded upon by his irritating relatives, like the Countess, continually nagging at him to marry money.

It would certainly bring the estate back to the glory it once had with of course all the modern trappings which undoubtedly would be exceedingly expensive.

The only way they suggested that money could be found was when it was attached to some rich woman who was desperate to become a Duchess.

If they had told him quite frankly, he had nothing to offer except his title he would actually have respected them for it, but they always tried to make it sound as if the only reason he was marrying was for an heir.

Somehow it cheapened everything.

He had brushed them aside over the last five years when he had spent so much time travelling or in London.

And he had indeed tried to believe that somehow things would change for the better and when he returned, he would find the need for money was not so urgent as it had seemed before he left.

He knew after he had spoken to his employees this morning that matters were worse than he expected.

Once again he was confronted with endless debts that had to be paid and the unavoidable question was still *how*.

Because he did not speak, the Countess regarded his back for a long time and then she tried to coax him,

"Be sensible, Alpin. You know we all love you and you have so much to offer the world, but it is impossible to do so when one is completely naked. Wake up to reality and realise that here is a tremendous opportunity – "

The Duke did not answer her nor did he turn round.

The Countess rambled on,

"Mary-Lee is such a sweet girl and her family is one of the most respected and influential in New York. At the same time they are so very rich that I don't think they even know themselves how much they possess."

She gave a little laugh before she added,

"But of course every rich American today respects a title. And if you don't snatch up Mary-Lee quickly, then undoubtedly there will be quite a number of my friends and acquaintances who are even more in need of the cash than you are!"

The Duke moved from the window and walked to where his cousin was sitting.

He stood looking at her for a moment or two and then he sat down beside her.

"I suppose I should be grateful," he said, "that you are interested enough in me as a man. I also like to believe you are fond of me regardless of my position as Head of the family."

"I have always loved you since you were a little boy, Alpin, but because you were an only child your father and mother naturally spoilt you and let you have your own way. I, as you know, was married off to David as soon as I was old enough to leave school because he was to inherit a title."

"Surely you loved him?" the Duke interposed.

"I felt for him what I thought was love, having no experience of it in any way. On the whole we have been very happy and, as you know, David is a charming person and it would be difficult not to be fond of him."

She sighed for a moment and then went on,

"Equally it was not the fairy tale love I am sure you are dreaming about."

"I had no idea, Cousin Moira. I always thought you and David had fallen in love at first sight and that yours was the ideal marriage all our relatives wanted to copy."

"And quite rightly so. We have been happy, but I am just telling you that is what you can find quite easily. It is really useless to go on hoping that the skies will open and some angel will drop into your arms and you feel you cannot live without her."

"Do you think that is what I am doing?" the Duke asked her with a twist to his lips.

"Of course you are, my dear Alpin. You have had the chance in the last six or seven years of marrying quite a number of beautiful young women who would also have provided you with the wherewithal you so urgently need for the Castle.

"In fact your mother and I were counting them up the other night and wondering why, like the Pharisee, you had passed by on the other side and left them to be snapped up by someone else."

The Duke did not answer and after a moment she added,

"I do know the answer. You are looking for love. The real love you read about in books."

She looked round as she spoke and threw out her hand towards the shelves that covered the whole of one wall.

"I have looked at some of these books and they all talk about a love a man finds once in a million years! You cannot expect to have everything in life, but that, Alpin, is exactly what you have been trying to find ever since you left school."

"What do you mean by that?"

"You are asking too much. You have your title, the Castle, the largest estate in the North of Scotland, and still you expect to find the love that may have inspired authors since man first began to write, but which is not practical in modern living and is seldom found by those who seek it – *very* very seldom if it comes to that."

"Yet it is something," the Duke said slowly, "that everyone wants deep down in their hearts."

"Just as everyone wants to be a millionaire! But it only happens to a very few people. It is ridiculous for you to believe when you have so much that you can sit back and demand even more."

"Now you really are depressing me, Cousin Moira."

"No, I am not. I am trying to make you see sense. It is good sense for you to marry Mary-Lee whilst she is still bemused by your title and your Castle. After that you can make her, because she is so young, become exactly as you want her to be and that is where we will all help you."

The Duke reflected that the one thing he would not want was his relatives, even his mother, interfering with his wife, but he thought it would be inappropriate to say so aloud.

He therefore sat back thinking that whilst he had never talked so frankly with his cousin before, he found it rather embarrassing to continue the conversation.

"There is no need for you to hurry yourself over this," she was saying. "But I want you to be really sensible for once and understand that the condition of everything around you cannot be neglected for ever."

The Duke wanted to argue, but she carried on,

"The sooner you make up your mind that marriage is the only way out for you, the sooner you will realise that here is a tremendous opportunity that may not come again, in meeting and marrying the lovely Mary-Lee. She is not only a millionairess but a very sweet and charming girl and that, I can assure you, my dear Alpin, is true."

There was a long pause before the Duke responded,

"I can only thank you for being so frank with me, and I will certainly consider everything you have said."

The Countess gave a cry of delight.

"That is just what I wanted you to say. Oh, Alpin, do be sensible over this. Your mother is terrified that you will let such an opportunity pass. She knows better than I do how much money is wasted on the estate and how your debt at the bank is reaching unmanageable heights."

The Duke disliked discussing his private affairs, but she prattled on regardless,

"Just as it is impossible for you to go on running up heavier bills every time you go off to London or travel abroad."

The Duke knew this was more or less true, but he had closed his eyes to it.

He also disliked, although he found it hard to say so, that the Countess, who after all was only his cousin, should know so much about his bank balance.

At the same time he was sensible enough to know that when his mother was alone in the Castle, it would be better that she talked to a relative than to someone who was just a friend.

"Very well, Cousin Moira," he said, "I will think over very seriously what you have said to me and, while I make no promises, I will certainly look further into the position we are in financially and what money is necessary for the estate itself."

"I feel sure you will be sensible, my dear Alpin."

She was gazing as she spoke at the very fine picture hanging over the fireplace.

"Of course there are things to sell in the Castle as you well know, although it would be terrible if there was nothing left for your son when he inherits.

"I remember your father almost crying when he had to part with the huge picture that used to hang in the hall. It had been there for over a hundred years, but the offer he received for it was so large he felt he could not refuse."

She gave a little laugh before she added,

"I was very young at the time, but as it was taken down I remember he said, 'if those damned Vikings had not carted away all our treasures when the Castle was first built, I would not have to sell this Van Dyck which breaks my heart'.

"'The Vikings are all dead, Uncle Donald,' I said to him, 'and a good thing too,' your father replied. 'May they rot in hell where they have undoubtedly taken the treasures they looted from this Castle'."

The Countess smiled before she finished,

"I have always remembered those words and every time anyone has mentioned the Vikings, I thought of them sitting on the glorious treasures they had carted away from the Castle, although I suspect what they valued far more than the gold goblets were the pretty village girls who were spirited away in their ships and were never seen again!"

The Duke laughed as if he could not help it.

"It's all very well blaming the Vikings, but I think some of my ancestors were indeed spendthrifts and that, of course, is why you should think I have inherited everything bad from them."

"That is just not true. You are as handsome, Alpin dear, as all your family have been. I have always thought that the reason you are so tall and your eyes so blue is that you have Viking blood in you."

"Nonsense," the Duke tried to protest.

"Quite a lot of the Scots from this part of Scotland have the same characteristics and where else could they have come from except in the great ships that swept across the North Sea to invade us."

The Duke chuckled.

"I have been told all this before, Cousin Moira, and it has always amused me. All right I am a Viking, and I reserve a Viking's right of choosing the woman I want and stealing her away from her home and perhaps her country!"

The Countess gave a cry and threw up her hands.

"You are not suggesting that you might marry a foreigner?"

"I thought that was what you were suggesting!"

The Countess dropped her hand and exclaimed,

"Of course I am. Except that I never think of the Americans as being foreigners. I was in fact thinking of those who speak a different language from ours like the Norwegians or Swedes, in addition the French with whom you spend so much of your time."

"Now you are making it even more difficult than it was when you started to preach to me, Cousin Moira."

His eyes were twinkling and he was only teasing.

The Countess gave a cry.

"I could not bear it if you brought home a French, German or Spanish wife. How could they be anything but alien up here in the Castle in the North of Scotland? The same would certainly apply to the Scandinavian countries, even though Princess Alexandra has proved to be a most charming and excellent wife for the Prince of Wales. But no one really thinks of her as a foreigner."

"I think from what you have been saying that you manipulate the world into what suits you rather than what it is. As I have already promised you, Cousin Moira, I will think over all you have said and consider it very carefully."

"What you have to realise, Alpin," she said firmly, "is that however you may try to talk yourself out of the fix you are in, you will have to be married and the sooner the marriage takes place the better. I assure you that every one of your relatives will say the same thing?"

"I can well believe it," the Duke sighed.

"Whilst you have been away," the Countess went on, "they have been deciding that each one of them should talk to you seriously and make you aware that you have to do something immediately to save the Castle, which means so much to all of us."

Now she was speaking in a different tone of voice.

The Duke stared at her in amazement.

There was a hard expression in his eyes and his lips tightened.

"You have now said your piece, Cousin Moira," he replied. "Therefore let's leave it at that. If you will excuse me, I have a message which I must send at once to one of the river watchers who will be out on duty on the river this afternoon."

He left the room as he finished speaking.

The Countess gave a deep sigh.

She knew she had made a mistake in saying that the other members of the family would also be talking to him and yet she did feel that he must realise how serious things were and how disastrous it was to carry on the way he was going at present.

'Perhaps I said too much,' she mused reflectively to herself as she walked across the room.

Then, as she opened the door, she muttered beneath her breath,

'The sooner he faces the truth the better. He has to listen to us!'

*

The Duke did not walk down to look for the river watcher.

Instead he climbed up the stairs and into one of the towers at a corner of the Castle.

From it he knew he would have a magnificent view of the sea on one side and his large estate on the other and he had always believed that up on the tower he was higher than anyone else in the County.

As he looked out to sea, he thought, as he had so often thought before, that nothing could be more glorious, his garden below him and the bay reaching out on either side.

The heather was turning purple on the moors and the strange lights which were only to be found in the far North made both the land and sea part of Fairyland.

Then he turned round to look to the North and then finally to the West and realised that he could see right over his own land and into the land owned by the MacFallins.

He had never really thought about it before.

But beyond the loch and a small forest of trees he could see the roof of the Earl of MacFallin's house.

It had never been a castle, but always the seat of the Chieftain of the MacFallin Clan.

'It's extraordinary,' the Duke now ruminated, 'how our two Clans have loathed and despised each other all down the centuries.'

Yet they continued living side by side and insulting each other in every way they possibly could.

And against all the traditions he had actually helped a MacFallin this morning to poach one of his own salmon!

He had found her as ordinary and as pleasant as any other Scot he might have encountered in the same way.

How could the feud have lasted for so many years?

Looking back he remembered there had been some frightful row at the Battle of Culloden when Bonnie Prince Charles had inadvertently placed them side by side.

The Chieftain of the McBaren Clan had accused the Chieftain of the MacFallins of taking over his place on the battlefield. In fact the two Clans had begun to fight each other rather than wait for the enemy, which was naturally the English.

They had been supported by the Chiefs of another Clan, and Prince Charles himself had apologised for the mistake that had been made.

Nevertheless the anger and fury the incident had aroused between the Clans had continued until long after the Prince of the Stuarts had escaped to exile in France, leaving Scotland to face its greatest enemy, the English.

'How could they have been so foolish?' the Duke wondered again.

He thought of how many Englishwomen he had found so delightful and how gratifyingly ardent they were when it came to lovemaking.

In fact he had enjoyed being in London perhaps more than in any other Capital City he had visited.

France had been fascinating, but his time there had been spent almost exclusively with *courtesans* who were entrancing yet expensive.

In London he only moved in the circle of those who clustered round the Prince of Wales.

He had been a visitor to many of the great houses of England and found them comfortable and civilised in the same way as he wished for his own Castle in Scotland.

He could not help wondering if the present Earl of MacFallin was as cultivated as his contemporaries were in England.

It had been his father's idea that he should go to an English school – Eton and then on to Oxford University.

It was natural therefore that he should speak perfect English with no trace of a Scottish accent.

Although he had been reluctant to admit it, he had English ideas of what should and should not be done rather than those that came from his ancestry.

He had the idea, although he did not actually know, that the Earl of MacFallin was very Scottish. Not only in his blood but in his behaviour and his ideas.

'I have progressed,' he said to himself, 'owing to the fact that the majority of my friends are English. Yet I am exceedingly proud of being a Scot, and would never do anything that is contrary to the beliefs and traditions of my people and my heritage.'

It was one thing to think like that, but another to carry it out.

He knew that if he really loved his own people as much as he thought he did, the houses on the estate should be repaired and the schools should be brought up-to-date.

There was no closing his eyes to the fact that a great number of men on his vast estate were living more or less from hand to mouth.

He turned away petulantly to look not inland but once again at the sea.

He knew in his heart that what the Countess had been saying to him was commonsense.

Sooner or later he would have to marry.

CHAPTER THREE

The guests at the dinner party that night were all neighbours whom the Duke had known for years.

They were very delighted, as they always were, to be invited to the Castle.

He talked to two of the ladies who told him long stories of how many salmon they had caught on various local rivers.

The men talked mostly of their particular piece of moorland and whether the grouse season would be good or bad this year.

The young people were talking noisily at the other end of the room and he hardly gave them a glance.

He was still feeling uneasy, as he dressed in his kilt, that he must do something for the Clan, even if it meant finally giving up his freedom.

Yet every instinct in his body revolted against the idea of marrying a woman just because she had money.

When Rory announced that dinner was served, they moved into the dining room.

The Duke naturally expected to sit with the most distinguished of his neighbours.

And to his astonishment he found that while he had an elderly lady of sixty on his right hand side, Mary-Lee was sitting on his left.

He suspected that either his mother or the Countess had deliberately changed the *placement* of the table.

When he had seen the *placement* earlier in the day, Mary-Lee was among the young at the far end of the table.

He recognised the fact that she was sitting next to him would create talk amongst the neighbours, and he was exceedingly annoyed that he had been unwittingly pushed into a position where his guests would be looking at him questioningly.

'Damn it,' he said to himself, 'I will not be bullied or pressured into doing something I don't want to do!'

He therefore talked animatedly to the elderly lady on his right and she was delighted with his attention.

She related all the gossip of their part of Scotland while he had been away.

There was, however, a gentleman on the other side of Mary-Lee who obviously appreciated young girls.

When the Duke glanced in their direction, he found he was flirting with her. He made her laugh and brought a colour into her cheeks.

After dinner the older guests, including the Duke, played bridge, while the young ones went to the music room and danced where someone was playing the piano.

The Duke did not know that this had been arranged, but he knew there was a woman from the village who was inevitably asked to every party, whether in the Castle or in the public house – she was an exceedingly good pianist and an expert in playing Scottish reels.

The Duke, when he sat down at the bridge table, was quite certain that Mary-Lee would be taught Highland dancing and doubtless would soon be proficient at it.

All evening he avoided the reproachful look in the Countess's eyes that told him she was most upset that he had ignored Mary-Lee throughout dinner nor had he made any effort to join the young in the music room.

Knowing that she would want to scold him when his visitors left, he saw them off at the front door.

Then going upstairs he kissed his mother goodnight on her way to her bedroom and before the Countess could say one word he left the party for his own room.

Although he was feeling tired, he found it hard to sleep.

He kept turning over in his mind again and again all that the Countess had said to him.

While he recognised that she had accurately made the situation very clear, he felt it was impossible for him to do what she demanded of him.

He would be bowing to *her* will and ignoring his own.

'If there is one thing I absolutely loathe,' he told himself, 'it's being manipulated and that is exactly what Cousin Moira is doing to me right now.'

*

Because he found it so difficult to sleep and when he did he had a nightmare, he woke early.

It was five o'clock in the morning when he finally slipped out of the house without anyone noticing.

Taking his rod and gaff he set off for the river.

It took some time to walk up to the place where he had met Sheinna the day before.

He usually started fishing near the Castle and the mouth of the river and this meant that if he was lucky, the fresh salmon were easier to catch.

At times there were great shoals of them leaping in the pools almost in unison.

However he had promised Sheinna that he would meet her upstream and he thought it would be interesting to fish the water close to the MacFallin's part of the river.

It would prevent *his* fish, as he thought of them, moving up into the enemy's water.

When he started to fish, it was nearly six o'clock and he thought that if Sheinna did join him an hour later there would still be time to help her have a catch or two before anyone else was about.

There was one thing that really infuriated him as he walked up the river.

This was the obvious marks left by the poachers the night before and he knew the lie of the river too well not to recognise where the net had been thrown across the most promising pool.

Footprints in the soft ground told him that there had been at least four men working the net and snatching the fish coming in from the sea.

'Where were the river watchers?' he asked himself angrily.

But he knew the answer only too well – they were growing old and now found it exceedingly unpleasant to encounter the poachers if it came to fisticuffs.

He had already learned that one river watcher had had his nose broken while he was away. Another had been kicked on the leg so viciously that it was a week before he was back at work on the banks.

Trying not to think how much he needed more river watchers as they were expensive, he threw out his line.

He had only been fishing for five minutes before he felt a soft pull on his line.

As he struck, the fish fought wildly to get away and it gave him a thrill that nothing else could ever do.

The fish jumped again and again until finally he drew it into the bank and gaffed it expertly.

It was only a five-pounder, but he was delighted with his catch.

Having seen that it was completely dead he covered it with leaves to keep away the flies and started to fish again.

He was in the process of landing his third fish when he heard someone clapping hands as he brought it ashore.

He saw it was Sheinna standing on the river bank only a few yards from him. He had been concentrating on his fish and had not heard her approaching.

"Is that the first one you have caught today?" she asked.

"No, the third," he replied proudly.

"You are hogging it before I even arrived!" Sheinna complained.

He was about to protest when she added,

"I must admit, I came here early, hoping I would catch one before you arrived."

The Duke laughed.

"Well, come and catch one now and I just hope that no one sees us."

It took a little time, but she managed to catch two while the Duke caught one more.

He found it difficult to fish himself whilst he was landing Sheinna's salmon.

As they sat down on the bank, the Duke remarked,

"I suppose, unless we want to be seen together, we should return home as the time is now approaching seven o'clock."

"I would love to catch half-a-dozen more before I leave," Sheinna exclaimed.

"Now *you* are being greedy. It's always the same with fishermen – they can never catch enough."

"For me this is the most exciting sport in the world, Your Grace, and I particularly want to be cheered up this morning."

"Why?" the Duke quizzed her.

She was silent for a moment and her head sank.

"It is what my father said to me last night – "

"And what was that?"

"I could hardly believe it myself. I lay awake most of the night thinking it was just a nightmare."

"What has happened, Sheinna?" he asked her again.

"Papa told me last night that he wants me to marry Sir Ewen Kiscard whose estate, as you will probably know, joins with ours a long way away."

The Duke thought carefully for a moment and then he remarked,

"Sir Ewen Kiscard is an old man."

"I know he is, but Papa thinks if his land is united with ours it would be very good for us and the Clan would be delighted to be larger and stronger."

"If I am not mistaken, Sir Ewen is getting on for seventy."

"That is right, Your Grace, but my Papa desires his land and Sir Ewen wants an heir."

The Duke stared at her and then he erupted,

"Of course you cannot marry a man who is nearly seventy. How old are you?"

"I am twenty, nearly twenty-one," she answered.

"Then he is old enough to be your grandfather. I have never heard of anything so patently ridiculous."

"But you do see," she said, "that Papa is thinking of the Clan and how nice it would be for them to become far

51

larger than we are now. As I have already said, Sir Ewen is not thinking of me but of having a son of his own."

"Whatever Sir Ewen thinks or does not think," the Duke replied sternly, "you must make it quite clear to your father that you do not intend to marry someone you don't love."

"That is exactly what I tried to tell him. I want to fall in love with a man for no reason except that I feel he is wonderful and that he loves me."

The Duke thought that he might be saying the same about himself and then he looked straight into Sheinna's gloriously blue eyes.

"You must be very firm about this."

"I will certainly try to be, Your Grace. At the same time Papa says I have to marry whoever he has chosen for me. And of course in the old days marriages were always arranged amongst the Clans."

"They were arranged for the advantage of the Clan, not for the happiness of those who had to do it and it is just appalling to contemplate that you should be pressured into marrying an old man. If I am right, I believe also that Sir Ewen has rather an unpleasant life-story."

"He has had two wives already," Sheinna sighed. "They both died and I cannot help feeling it was because he was unkind to them."

"How can your father be so ridiculous as to even believe that you might marry a man like him?"

"He wants me to become important in the County and to be the Mistress of Sir Ewen's land. I am terrified, seriously terrified, I will not be able to stand up to him."

The Duke thought he might be saying that himself after the way the Countess had behaved yesterday.

"You must run away – " he suggested aloud.

Sheinna made a helpless gesture with her hands.

"Where to?" she asked. "I was so very happy when I was living with my grandmother, but now that I am home everything is different and I am afraid because Papa and Sir Ewen are so strong. I am beginning to realise I cannot even think for myself."

She spoke in a voice that made the Duke feel she really was helpless.

He knew only too well that, as Chieftain of a Clan, the Earl was a very overpowering and distinguished figure – almost like a King to the people who bore his name.

In fact the Duke now remembered that his father had often told him that the Earl was a dangerous man.

He was determined to exert traditional power and authority over all his Clansmen and he expected them to admire his strength and to be willing to be led by him.

"If we were living a century earlier," the Duke's father had said, "I am quite certain that MacFallin would be leading an Army of his men against us and we would be fighting for our lives from first thing in the morning until last thing at night."

The Duke had laughed at the time, but now he felt that his father was undoubtedly right.

This young, innocent and pretty girl would have no chance of standing up against him.

"What can I do?" Sheinna asked in a broken voice. "What *can* I do?"

"You must run away," the Duke advised her again decisively.

She made another helpless gesture with her hands.

"But where can I go?"

The Duke thought for a moment.

"I have an idea which you may think is quite mad. I am not certain whether I am suggesting an answer to your problem or letting off a bomb."

"I don't understand. Tell me what you are saying?" Sheinna begged.

The Duke paused again before replying,

"As it happens I am in very much the same position as you. I am being pressured by my relatives into marrying a young girl simply because she is very rich."

"But then surely, Your Grace, *you* don't have to do anything you don't want to do."

The Duke smiled.

"I am being badgered, even as you are, until it is very difficult for me to refuse, simply because money is needed, not for me personally, but for the Castle, the estate, and of course the Clansmen, including river watchers."

"I thought, because you were so important, you had everything you wanted," said Sheinna. "Although I have only just passed by it, nothing could be more magnificent than your ancestral Castle."

"It needs a lot of money to be spent on it and if I tell you the truth, I am very much in debt."

"So they want you to marry a rich wife?" Sheinna questioned.

"They want me to marry a young girl who will find me too old for her and whom I will eventually find boring."

"But you are a man – a Duke. Surely you could just refuse."

"It is not as easy as it sounds. They are appealing to me to save my home, my people and all those who look to me to save their sheep and cattle which are plundered just because we are not strong enough to resist those who covet them."

"So you feel," Sheinna said in a very small voice, "that you have to sacrifice yourself for the Clan."

"That is exactly what they want me to do, just as they want you to strengthen your Clan by marrying a man old enough to be your grandfather."

"I cannot do it," cried Sheinna. "I cannot! Please, please help me and tell me how I can hide from them. But even if I do, I feel sure they will find me."

"You cannot run away alone, have you no relations or friends in England or abroad who would welcome you if you asked them for help?"

"I suppose they would let me stay with them," she said hesitatingly, "but Papa would soon find me and insist on my going back home."

The Duke thought that was very likely and as she was young and pretty, she would not be hard to trace.

There was a poignant silence and then the Duke remarked,

"I am thinking of a way of escape for you and for myself, but it's difficult to put it into words."

"Oh, tell me, tell me anything," Sheinna begged. "I am really desperate. To be honest I would rather die than marry an old man looking like Sir Ewen. Papa told me that he finds it hard to find any attractive women in this part of Scotland, who will put up with him, being, as he is, so old and ugly."

"I am thinking, Sheinna, of something which would make your father think again and that would infuriate my relations. But neither of them could do anyhing about it."

"What are you talking about?"

The Duke smiled.

"I must sound as if I am talking nonsense, but I am really thinking it out in my own mind. *You* are in trouble and *I* am in trouble. We are both under the same pressure – to marry someone we have no wish to marry."

"That is true enough, Your Grace, but how can we refuse? You can run away, but I, as a mere woman, would soon be caught and brought back in disgrace and probably in chains as well!"

"Well, we have to give them other issues to think about rather than the marriages they have arranged for us," the Duke said. "Therefore what I am suggesting, Sheinna, and you may think it very strange, is that we pretend that we have fallen in love and want to marry one another!"

She turned to look at him in sheer astonishment.

Her eyes were very large in her small pointed face.

"I just don't understand," she whispered after what seemed a very pregnant silence.

"It's quite simple," the Duke persisted. "I will say that I want to marry you as it is now time this ridiculous feud between our two Clans came to an end."

There was silence before Sheinna exclaimed,

"My father would have a stroke at the idea of any MacFallin marrying a McBaren!"

"Of course he would and my own Clan would feel exactly the same. That is why, in giving them something else to think about and argue over, we will gain some time to settle our lives our own way. You could find someone you love and who loves you – and I could do the same."

He paused for a moment before adding,

"It is something I have been trying to do for some time but have so far failed."

Sheinna looked pensive and then responded,

"There are two things that might then happen. My father might make me marry Sir Ewen at once in order to rescue me from your clutches or he might force the Clans into actually fighting each other. I could not bear to see any of our people killed or wounded."

"I feel the same, Sheinna, but if we are fortunate they will quickly call a truce. By the time that happens Sir Ewen will have withdrawn from the contest because it does not concern him or he could find someone else to marry."

To his surprise Sheinna giggled.

"This cannot be true – it sounds exactly like a story out of a book. You know as well as I do that my father and his friends will rage against the McBarens as they always have, while your people will undoubtedly do the same."

"Of course they will, but while they are doing so they will forget about the marriages they had arranged for us and we will remain unmarried and for a time at least not under any pressure – "

He paused before he continued slowly,

"It will give us time to look around to find people who are more interesting than those we meet every day."

Sheinna clasped her hands together.

"You make it sound as if it is possible," she sighed, "but I cannot help thinking you are being optimistic. It's really absurd to think that we could defy all the centuries in which the MacFallins have always hated the McBarens."

"They will talk and they will talk, but I would very much doubt if they will take really violent action. But they will try to make it quite clear that we are unsuited to each other and, however much we plead with them, they will not allow us to marry."

"Do you think while they are doing that," Sheinna asked, "you might find the woman you really love and I might find a man who will really love me?"

"It's a chance worth trying, Sheinna, but in every race an outsider sometimes wins!"

She laughed.

"It's a fantastic idea, Your Grace, but do you really think we dare do anything quite so outrageous?"

"I am prepared to try it if you are, Sheinna. What I suggest is that this afternoon I send a carriage to ask you to come over to the Castle for tea to meet my mother and my cousin. When you see the effect that bombshell will have on them, you will have some idea what the shock will be like to your father when I tell him why I am calling on him after all these years!"

"He will not believe you are real, so *please*, please, Your Grace, do you really mean it? It just sounds to me so extraordinary and outrageous, but, as you suggest, it may take my father's mind off my marrying Sir Ewen."

"That is the whole idea," the Duke murmured.

"And doubtless your family will be so occupied in getting rid of me they will forget for the time being that they are pushing you into marrying someone else."

"They have begged me to marry and I will tell them I am obeying them," the Duke chuckled. "I shall point out that it is time the feud between our two Clans came to an end. Between us we could be a formidable force together against any other Clan and also against the poachers of our salmon and the dastardly cattle-thieves."

"Oh, it's impossible! I know it's impossible," cried Shienna. "But it's like an exciting story which you never know how it will end until you reach the last page."

"We have a long way to go before we reach our goal, but as long as it will stop, as far as I am concerned, at least temporarily, the eternal nagging from my relatives, and save you from what you quite rightly suggest would be a fate worse than death."

"But can we really win?" Sheinna asked nervously.

"I have told you what I think we should do. I will send a carriage for you at half-past-three. I think it would be wise if you don't say where you are going until I return with you."

"That will be quite easy, because I know that Papa is going out later this afternoon to talk things over with Sir Ewen. It will take him at least three quarters of an hour to get there and if they talk for an hour, then three quarters of an hour to come back."

"That certainly gives us breathing space," the Duke commented dryly. "As I have just said, the carriage will arrive for you at half-past-three by which time your father will undoubtedly be miles away."

"Then we will be temporarily free and it will give us time, as you have said, to look around and meet other people. Although I enjoyed living with my grandmother, she did not know many young gentlemen."

She looked up at the Duke as she added,

"I did attend a few dances in London, but I did not make many friends of my own age because we were so often travelling or else I was at school."

"Well, you are now going to have every chance, if I arrange it cleverly, to meet all the young men on this side of the County. There were several dining with me at the Castle last night who were intelligent and charming. You would doubtless feel the same about them."

"It all sounds wonderful, Your Grace, but I am only afraid that Papa will try to shoot you or the MacFallins will march on the Castle and attempt to destroy it!"

"They have tried to do that in the past and failed. In fact I think the guns we pointed at them are still up in the turrets. When you come to the Castle, we shall look for them and see if they still work!"

"I suppose," Sheinna said after a moment's silence, "I am awake and not dreaming."

"You look very much awake to me," he answered her with a smile, "and don't forget you have caught two salmon."

"I must take them home and delight Papa with them while he is at breakfast. Please help me carry them to the road. I have told one of our grooms to come and collect me about now."

"That was an excellent idea, Sheinna, and we had better walk first onto your ground so that you are not seen coming up to the road from mine."

"You think of everything, Your Grace, and thank you, thank you for thinking of me."

She kept her hand on his arm and then continued,

"I am not sure it will work and I am more than half afraid that Papa will merely laugh, and force me up the aisle with Sir Ewen before I can say a definite 'no'."

"He cannot do that without a Special Licence. I am sure that when you do get married, he will want to stage a celebration so that all the Clansmen can take part."

"That is true. In fact I think he is already planning the huge feast he will give for his guests at my 'wedding breakfast', as we call it in Scotland."

"Which you are certainly not going to have with Sir Ewen. Try not to be afraid. Unless I am much mistaken they will talk endlessly and will still be doing so when we are too old to think of being married and are about to be carried into the graveyard!"

Sheinna laughed as he meant her to.

"Now what I have promised you," the Duke said, picking up their salmon, "is that you will meet a lot of charming young men from this part of the County as well as my friends from London whom I intend to ask to stay at the Castle."

"How can you be so kind and how can I ever thank you enough, Your Grace?"

"Really, I am thinking of us both," he answered. "They have been nagging at me ever since I came home. Quite frankly I am sick to death of being told who I should marry and why I should do so. If I had any pride left, I would run away to America and make my fortune there as others have done."

Even as he thought of America, a picture of Mary-Lee formed in his mind.

He was sure that his cousin would now be singing his praises to her and making it quite clear that she must marry him.

'She has no wish to marry me and I have no wish to marry her,' he told himself firmly.

They walked in silence until they were out of the Duke's ground and onto the MacFallin's.

"I am not coming any further," the Duke said, "just in case I am seen, but if your fish are too heavy for you, I should leave them under a bush or a tree and send one of your servants to collect them later."

"In the meantime they might be stolen," Sheinna replied, "so I will just leave my rod, which I assure you is not so precious as these salmon I have caught myself with only a little help from you."

The Duke laughed.

"You must take all the credit and make sure your father has no idea that we know each other until we return this afternoon telling him what we intend to do. I am quite sure it will go off like grapeshot!"

"I would not be surprised if the house falls down on our heads, but thank you again for helping me, even if the sensation we cause turns out to be even more calamitous than we anticipate."

"If nothing else it will give them something to talk about. If the story finishes in a proper fairytale manner, Sir Ewen will marry Mary-Lee and they will live happily ever after!"

Sheinna laughed at the idea and because the sound was so infectious the Duke laughed too.

"We are doing nothing wrong," he said almost as if he was reassuring himself, "and I am more than certain that eventually a great deal of good will come from it."

"I shall pray it will," Sheinna murmured.

"I was thinking only the other day," he added, "how ridiculous these old feuds between our Clans are. It is time we thought first of Scotland and be determined to make it more prosperous and up-to-date than it is at present."

"I think it is a lovely, lovely country and I am very proud to be a part of it," Sheinna insisted.

"I feel the same," the Duke answered, "but I can also see Scotland's faults and just how far it is behind the times. So you and I have to wake it up and make it realise there are a great many new ideas and new problems which the Scots must tackle on their own."

They came to a large tree and Sheinna propped her rod against it.

"Whoever I send for this should be able to find it," she said. "And thank you once again for being so kind. If, when you return home, you change your mind about what we will do, just send me a note."

She paused before she carried on,

"But I will be praying you will not do so, because I am so scared that I will find myself married to Sir Ewen even before I have bought my trousseau."

"Whatever else we do, we have to get rid of him. Goodbye, Sheinna, until this afternoon and I will be very upset if the carriage comes back without you."

"It will certainly not do that," she promised.

She smiled at him as she walked away carrying a salmon in each hand.

The Duke watched her until she was nearly out of sight and then he went back to the river to collect his rod and the three salmon he had caught.

It was only as he was walking towards the Castle that he wondered if he had not been rather mad.

He had suggested an extraordinary way of escape both for Sheinna and himself.

Would it work?

Equally he was genuinely horrified at the idea of any young girl being married to Sir Ewen.

He remembered his father saying that Sir Ewen was a serious disgrace to his family and to Scotland. The way he pursued young women and the scandals he caused were shocking.

The Duke, however, had no intention of informing Sheinna as to just how unpleasant Sir Ewen was.

He thought that her father, the Earl, must have gone off his head if he could even contemplate allowing his only daughter to be married to such an old roué.

'It is something I could hardly tell the Earl when I have little or no acquaintance with him,' the Duke mused, 'but I can definitely do so when I arrive supposedly to ask for Sheinna's hand.'

As he walked on, he thought to himself how tired he was of his mother and the Countess continually nagging him – they were forcing him into a position with Mary-Lee from which he would find it very hard to extricate himself.

He felt sure that, if her father arrived unexpectedly in Scotland, his mother would tell him how fond her son was of Mary-Lee and she of him, and then it would be only a question of how soon he was pushed up the aisle to find himself married.

'Whatever the final result of this challenge of the McBarens to the MacFillans,' he told himself with a smile, 'it will at least release me from a yoke from America.'

As he strode on, he was whistling *The McBaren Call to Arms*.

When the Castle loomed up ahead, he thought how much it meant to him.

Maybe any sacrifice should be made to keep it as fine and impressive as it had always been all through the past centuries.

'My ancestors have all died for Scotland and our Clan,' he reflected. 'All I am being asked to do is to marry for the sake of those who bear my name and who follow on behind me – '

Just for a moment he was almost ashamed that he would not make the required sacrifice.

He indeed had just to accept the obvious solution of marrying Mary-Lee and not only would she be thrilled to accept him and his title but her father would be delighted.

He knew without his mother or his cousin saying so that unlimited money would be available for him to put in hand all the necessary repairs and to re-establish the whole of the great estate in proper order.

'It is what I ought to do and what I must do,' his head told him – but *not* his heart.

Then he remembered that he was not only trying to save himself but also Sheinna.

It was just unthinkable, completely and absolutely unthinkable, that she should be forced to marry Sir Ewen and it was appalling that her father, the Earl, seemed to be ignoring how unpleasant the old man was.

Yet he could understand.

He resented the MacFallins intruding on what had originally been his land.

They had reasoned for themselves that Sir Ewen's estate joined onto theirs and if the two were to be united by matrimony, the MacFallins would take a large step forward in influence and prestige.

In the North of Scotland at any rate they would be almost on equal terms with their old enemy, the McBarens.

'I must prevent that eventuality at any cost,' the Duke told himself, 'for the sake of my Clan.'

Then as he walked into the house, Rory, the butler, came running out to meet him.

"Your Grace made a good catch this morning!" he smiled taking the salmon from him.

"I was lucky," the Duke answered him modestly.

"Things be cheering up now Your Grace be home," Rory remarked, "and that be all that matters."

He disappeared with the salmon before the Duke could think of a suitable reply.

Then he told himself that, whatever they might say or think, he was behaving like a gentleman in refusing to marry an American just because she proffered money.

That was the right way to lead his people and make them happy.

When he looked back at his childhood, he could remember how happy his father and mother were together and how the Castle seemed to be filled with laughter and light.

'One day that is what we will have again,' he told himself. 'Whatever people may say, love is something that cannot be bought and sold over the counter with money.'

He could almost feel his cousin Moira laughing at him.

Yet as he gazed out of the window at the bright sun shining on the sea he told himself again that what he really wanted more than anything was love.

Although it might take him years, he was quite sure that eventually he would find it.

CHAPTER FOUR

Sheinna returned home feeling very apprehensive.

Anything indeed was far better than being forced to marry Sir Ewen.

Yet she was only too aware that her father would be horrified at her saying she proposed to marry the Chieftain of the dreaded McBarens.

Ever since she had been old enough to talk, she was taught that the McBarens were bad and wicked people.

Her father and all his Clansmen hated them.

As she grew older she wondered why they were so violent about them. She was told that they had fought one another for generations.

And nothing would stop them now from looking on the McBarens as their greatest enemy.

Then she had gone to England and found there were no Clans there. Men and women became friends with all different sorts of people and not only with those they were related to by name or blood.

She had, as she lived with her grandmother, grown up to feel tolerant towards almost everyone and it had been the same when she visited France.

Of course there were those who were snobbish and who thought people who had titles were superior beings, but on the whole most people accepted those they met at their face value.

Sheinna actually found herself exceedingly popular with everyone she came into contact with.

"The Clans are out of date," she had once said to her grandmother, who had laughed and replied,

"You will not find it so in Scotland. Your father is convinced that he is the King of his own Clan and he will not have anyone interfering with him."

Sheinna had laughed heartily at the time, but when she came home she found that it was only too true.

Her father considered himself of great importance and he expected all the Clansmen who bore his name and over whom he ruled to obey and respect him dutifully.

Sheinna had often laughed to herself and felt that her father expected her to curtsy to him when they met!

He was furious if anyone omitted to address him as 'my Lord'.

Of course she was proud of her family, which went back for many generations and she had read the history of the MacFallins and was impressed by all that the various Earls who preceded her father had achieved.

Equally she guessed that the MacFallins were not of any particular significance among the other Clans. There were many Highland Chieftains more distinguished than her father.

She had, however, done her very best to behave as he would like and she had always listened obediently to his endless stories of the battles the MacFallins had fought and always seemed to win.

Appreciating the fact that everyone surrounding her wore a kilt, it had at first seemed to her strange after being away so long.

She was used to seeing the young men in England very smart in their evening dress and the French took great interest in their appearance and that of their women.

Living again in the MacFallin family house which was several centuries old was a new experience for her.

At first she found it very interesting but at the same time extremely uncomfortable and she missed the luxuries she had found in her grandmother's house in London and had enjoyed in Paris.

The cupboards, heavily made out of Scottish wood, were far too short for her gowns and the carpets in some rooms were threadbare, but they were considered much too precious to be removed because of their age.

It all, Sheinna felt, came down to the same custom.

If an item had been in the family for generations, it must be almost worshipped as if it was a sacred record of their achievements.

Her father, the Earl, liked things done in old style. The piper walked three times round the dining room table after dinner and was then rewarded with a dram of whisky.

To begin with Sheinna thought that this ritual was entertaining, but as it happened every evening, she began to find it boring and extremely noisy.

It lasted far too long because the Earl wanted the piper to play the best tunes for the pipes as well as the Lament and the *MacFallins' War Song* every night.

The Earl would sit back in his chair with a satisfied look on his face and Sheinna became increasingly aware that he took it as a personal tribute to himself, giving him a feeling of grandeur that nothing else could.

*

When Sheinna had bade farewell to the Duke by the river, she climbed up to the road and there coming towards her was a groom and the pony-cart to collect her.

The groom grinned at her when he saw that she was carrying two salmon.

"You've been real lucky, my Lady," he greeted Sheinna. "That'll please 'is Lordship."

"I'm sure he will think me very clever."

"That you were," the groom replied. "And you got 'em in without a gaff, my Lady, unless you left it behind."

Sheinna drew in her breath.

She had completely forgotten that she would either have a net or a gaff for the fish with her.

Of course the Duke had landed them for her.

Now because she was frightened of what the groom would think, she said quickly,

"Oh dear, I have left my net behind, Torquil, but I will go fishing again this afternoon and collect it then."

The groom grinned.

"Let's hope then you'll have plenty need of it, my Lady."

"That is just what I'm hoping too," replied Sheinna.

They drove on in silence and soon she could see the huge and somewhat ugly house ahead of her and then she thought how exciting it would be to see Barenlock Castle.

The groom drew the cart up outside the front door and as he did so, he enquired,

"Shall I takes the salmon to the kitchen, my Lady?"

"Yes, please do, Torquil, and thank you very much for fetching me," Sheinna replied.

The butler, who was waiting in the hall, asked her,

"Did your Ladyship have any luck?"

"Yes, I did, Donald," she answered. "Two lovely salmon and I hope we will have one to eat tonight."

"I'll tell cook, if that's what you be a-wantin', my Lady."

He spoke with a broad accent and she thought in his kilt he looked very unlike the suave smart butler who had presided over her grandmother's house, where the footmen had worn a trim livery.

She was also comparing the climb up the stairs to the dining room, which she had always considered totally unnecessary, but it was correct in large Scottish houses.

She preferred the large dining room on the ground floor, which had been filled with her grandmother's friends where the food was always delicious and, if the gentlemen were to be believed, the wine was even better.

She had only been back at her home for a very short while, but already she found the heavy meals provided by the Scottish cook monotonous and predictable.

If she compared them with all the wonderful dishes she had enjoyed in France, they were almost inedible.

Of course there was salmon and venison to eat and as they were near the sea there was fresh cod and mackerel, but she longed for the delicious Parisian sauces.

Whatever the Scots might brag about their venison, to Sheinna's taste there was nothing as good as spring lamb or a young chicken.

'I am a Scot and I really must not criticise my own people,' she had told herself over and over again.

But she could not pretend that she did not miss the elegance and comfort she had found South of the border.

When she entered the breakfast room, she found her father already seated at the top of the table.

"Where have you been?" he asked. "I was told you went out very early!"

"I went fishing," Sheinna replied simply.

"You should have asked me where you should go," her father said. "I know every pool in the river better than

I know my own name and I would have made sure you had a catch."

"As it happened I landed two."

"Two!" the Earl exclaimed. "Well, that *was* clever of you."

He spoke almost reluctantly as if he had no wish for her to achieve anything without his help and guidance.

Sheinna kissed his cheek before walking over to the sideboard, where she helped herself to the inevitable bowl of porridge.

Secretly she had no liking for porridge, but was afraid to say so.

However, she took as little as she could in the small wooden bowl that had been given to her at her Christening.

She knew her father in the correct Scottish manner had already eaten his porridge standing up and had put salt on it rather than sugar.

She sat down at the table to eat hers.

The tradition of men standing up to eat it had been handed down from generation to generation and it was in case, while eating their porridge, an enemy stabbed them in the back.

She could not help thinking that now in the security of his very own dining room, her father would be far more comfortable sitting rather than standing.

"Where did you catch the salmon?" he asked.

"I am not quite certain of the name of the pool," she responded. "But it was near to where our part of the river begins."

Her father made a sound which she knew was one of contempt.

"Keep away from that part of the water!" he cried.

"I have no wish to be told by the men who work for that absentee Duke that you were trespassing."

"If they had been there, they might have taken my fish away from me," Sheinna parried lightly.

"They would certainly have done so. If you ask me they often trespass on my land when they think there's no one about."

His voice sharpened as he went on,

"In fact I am almost certain that I saw one several evenings ago, but he disappeared before I could get near enough to tell him what I thought of him! I cannot move as quickly as I used to."

"I am sure that there's plenty of fish for everyone, Papa, without any of us being unpleasant about it."

"Unpleasant," her father exclaimed sharply. "I can assure you, if I see anyone poaching on my land, they will be lucky if they get away alive!"

He spoke with a violence which was characteristic of him.

Sheinna had always thought it was more bravado than anything else, but it told her all too clearly what he felt about the McBarens.

"What are you going to do today, Papa?" she asked.

"I have to go to the village later this morning. The Minister wants to see me about repairs to the Kirk and I have something else to discuss with him that will take a long time."

"What is that?" Sheinna asked him.

It was not because she was particularly curious, but she thought it polite to show an interest.

"Well, if you want the truth, it's your marriage," the Earl replied. "I was thinking in the night that it would be quite impossible to fit everyone into the Kirk, so I am wondering if we would be wiser to have the ceremony in a larger Kirk than the one here on our doorstep."

There was short silence before Sheinna burst out,

"I have already told you, Papa, I have no wish to be married. I have only just come home and I want to enjoy being with you. As I said yesterday, I will *not* marry Sir Ewen."

"You will do as you are told!" the Earl shouted at her, "and I will have no nonsense about it."

"He is old, he is horrible and if you insist on my marrying him, I will run away!"

The Earl laughed and it was not a pleasant sound.

"And where, my dear girl, would you go?"

"Where you could not find me," Sheinna replied.

"Then let me make it very clear that you will obey me as your father and the Chieftain of this fine Clan – "

The Earl paused for a moment before he added,

"I told you there was no hurry, but I need to talk things over with Sir Ewen. At the same time, since I am seeing the Minister about other matters, I will certainly be discussing your marriage."

His voice deepened as he carried on,

"And how to make it one of the most momentous and rousing events that the MacFallins have ever taken part in."

For a second Sheinna thought of screaming at him and insisting again that she would never marry anyone she did not love, especially such an old man as unattractive and repulsive as Sir Ewen.

Then she recalled that the Duke had a solution for her and himself and it would thus be a waste of breath.

She then put aside her bowl and in silence helped herself to one of the dishes on the sideboard.

The only habit in this house that echoed English manners was the way they helped themselves at breakfast, otherwise the servants waited on them at every meal.

"Now what I am planning," her father was saying, "is that you should have a large number of bridesmaids in attendance on you, which will naturally please our relations and our neighbours."

His voice was now quite pleasant as he rambled on,

"The Clan pipers will play you into the Kirk and play you out of it. They will also play almost continuously during the Reception."

Sheinna did not answer as she knew that her father was thinking aloud and even if she did make a comment, he was unlikely to pay any attention.

As it happened, despite the fact of having spent the night with very little sleep, after her exertions this morning she was feeling quite hungry.

Having finished the fish fillets, she helped herself to scones and butter from her father's farm.

"I suppose," the Earl was saying, "you will need a wedding gown. As the wedding will be a very large one, it must be very smart and spectacular.

"We have the veil which has been passed down the family for centuries and you will carry a bouquet of white heather which will undoubtedly bring good luck to your marriage."

Sheinna felt like screaming it would be unlucky. For anyone of her age to be married to a man who was so much older and, as she thought, exceedingly unpleasant, could in no way enjoy good luck.

But to argue with her father at this moment would do no good.

Again there was a poignant silence.

"I suppose," the Earl said after a long pause, "that you will want to go to Edinburgh for your wedding gown. Although I daresay there could easily be someone nearer who could supply you with one."

Sheinna mused that he was being far too optimistic.

No dressmakers, if there were any in the villages, would be able to supply the sort of gown her father was contemplating for her. She was quite certain that even in Edinburgh they would indeed not be as smart as anything she could be able to find in London or Paris.

She wondered if she insisted on going to either of these two Capitals to buy a wedding dress that her father would agree.

Then she recognised, as she had been speaking of running away, he would think it a trick on her part to evade the marriage.

As she made no further reply, he then rose from the table, saying,

"When I have seen the Minister, I will tell you what his suggestions are. If you are going fishing again, you are to be back by five o'clock and don't be late."

Having given his orders, he then stalked out of the dining room, closing the door noisily behind him.

Sheinna put her hands up to her face.

As she had told the Duke, she was frightened, more frightened now than she had ever been in her whole life.

It was so hard to visualise what might happen when she announced that she intended to marry the Duke.

It would certainly cause a terrible commotion.

Yet it would at least distract her father's attention from his present plans.

She walked slowly upstairs to her bedroom.

She suddenly felt half afraid that the Duke had only been playing with her.

Perhaps he really had no intention of declaring that they intended to marry each other.

Then she told herself that, if nothing else, he was a gentleman and he would not raise her hopes falsely on such a serious matter.

'He is in just the same difficulty as I am,' she told herself firmly. '*So he understands.*'

All the same she was only too well aware of how doubly furious her father would be when he found out that, after refusing to marry Sir Ewen, she had chosen to marry the enemy and bogeyman of her childhood – the Duke of Barenlock.

'I am sure the very idea,' she thought, 'will make him angrier than he has ever been.'

She looked back and remembered the times he had raged at her because she had done something wrong and punished her in what her mother had thought was a cruel fashion.

These punishments had usually ended in her mother being the heroine. She had brought her food secretly if her father had said she was to have nothing to eat for twenty-four hours.

And at other times her mother had prevented him from actually striking Sheinna.

But now her mother was dead.

And Sheinna wondered if anyone would be able to prevent him from punishing her now in some horrible way because she was defying him.

'If only Grandmama had not died, I would still be happy in London,' she murmured to herself.

Then, almost as if a voice was prompting her, she knew she had to be brave.

She was a MacFallin and her ancestors had won a great number of battles through their bravery.

She walked over to the window to gaze out at the mountains on the other side of the river and told herself that the Scots would never accept defeat and if nothing else she was a Scot.

However brave she was pretending to be, the hours passed very slowly.

Until she reckoned that the carriage to collect her would soon be waiting outside.

She changed into one of her smart gowns she had bought in Paris and on her head she placed the pretty hat that had been sold to go with it.

As she walked slowly downstairs, she thought the Duke would think she looked very different.

He had so far only seen her wearing a warm jumper over a tartan skirt and because she had come out fishing there had been no hat on her curly hair.

Her hair had been much admired in England and in France and was almost a speciality of Scotland because although it was fair there was a distinct touch of red in it.

It fell in natural cascading curls over her cheeks and her father had often complained it was not red enough.

But the young men who danced with her in London had congratulated her. She looked, they said, so beautiful that they found it hard to express their feelings in words.

Sheinna had laughed at all they said and had not taken them seriously, but she thought they had been very amusing in their own way.

They made all their compliments sound completely sincere and the Scots, she mused, would not be able to compete in that field.

This had been proved true since she had returned to Scotland. Her young relations who had come to meet her at her father's request were all rather gauche and also, she considered, poorly educated.

Half a century ago it had become a fashion for the older sons of the Chieftain of the Clan to be educated either in Edinburgh or in England and this policy had produced new and different young Scottish gentlemen.

They were smart, they were intelligent and they had travelled.

The owners of the castles and the big estates began to invite their English friends in August to stay with them for the grouse shooting and at the beginning of the summer they came for the salmon fishing.

It made the Scots, as the wits put it, 'pull up their socks' and it certainly made the young more entertaining and hospitable than they had been in the past.

What was more, instead of marrying the girls of another Clan, quite a number of Scots married English girls and such marriages were often most successful.

The English had been the enemy for many years, but as Scotland was now part of the United Kingdom, the English were accepted by the Scottish aristocracy, though they were still regarded with a healthy suspicion by the ordinary Clansmen.

Sheinna went downstairs to wait for the carriage the Duke had promised to send for her.

She was thinking as she did so that perhaps at the Castle she would meet some charming and sophisticated Englishman she could feel more at home with than with a Scot.

'If I could only fall in love with one,' she thought, 'and he with me, we could slip away to the South and live there happily for ever. And very very much more happily than I could ever live with someone like Sir Ewen.'

There was no one of the household downstairs.

So dressed as if she was going to a smart party in Mayfair, Sheinna regarded herself in the mirror.

She wondered what the Duke would think of her now and then she thought that his relations, if they were Scottish, would definitely think she was overdressed.

She felt that she must run back upstairs and change, but it was now too late.

As she hesitated, she heard a carriage drawing up outside.

It would be a mistake for anyone to find out where she was going and she was sure the butler and the other staff would be out or resting at this time, as they knew that her father would not be back until five o'clock when tea would be served.

She ran across the hall and opened the front door.

There was a smart closed carriage waiting outside drawn by two horses and the footman on the box realised who she was.

Without speaking he then opened the door of the carriage and Sheinna stepped into it.

As the footman climbed back onto the box of the carriage, the horses started off.

As far as she could tell, no one had seen her leave.

She sat back in the carriage, thinking it was very comfortable and indeed far more luxurious than the one her father used.

The horses too were very fast and although they could not hurry along the narrow road that ran more or less parallel with the river, Sheinna found herself wondering if the other horses the Duke had in the stables at his Castle were as fine as these.

Her father had always bought local roughly bred horses that were not in any way outstanding and yet they were tough and strong enough to cope with the roads when they were under snow and the moors when he went out to shoot.

Sheinna had ridden in Rotten Row.

Her grandmother's horses were all chosen for her by one of her relations and were all thoroughbreds, superb even amongst aristocratic owners.

Thinking it over as they travelled on, Sheinna was aware that her father was content with Scotland as it had always been.

But the Duke had lived to all intents and purposes in an entirely different world.

She had heard that he had been educated in England and had travelled extensively abroad and her father had always sneered at the young Scots who had done so.

"They should be content with their own country," he had thundered. "What could be better than the moors of Bonny Scotland with the glorious history of our fight for our independence?"

Sheinna had tried to understand his rather narrow patriotism and she had in fact respected him because he was so proud of his possessions and his family heritage.

Yet she had lived in England for years and she therefore found that the Scots, as she saw them now, were in many ways uncivilised.

They were clearly completely out of touch with the outside world which was developing fast and turning into an entirely new generation of people, producing new ships, new trains, machinery of every sort in what the Americans called 'a new age.'

To Sheinna it was all very exciting.

She read the newspapers avidly to find out about the new products that had just been invented and which countries were challenging one another in technology and innovation.

'That is a brave new world I will never make Papa understand,' she surmised as the carriage moved a little more quickly.

Then, when she thought of the grey hair and the faltering steps of Sir Ewen, she felt herself shiver.

The fear was back in her heart.

The carriage was now moving even more quickly because the road was smoother and, as they drove along the coast for a short while, she could see the sea.

Then she had a glimpse, when she was still half-a-mile away, of the Castle.

She had thought ever since she was a child it was the most romantic Castle she had ever seen.

Now with the sun shining on its high turrets and glittering on the sea beneath it, it looked almost unreal – as if the scene had stepped out of Fairyland.

As the road turned inland they passed through a small village and now she could only see the high purple moors that loomed above the Castle.

Then they reached the great gates.

Just for a moment Sheinna felt scared, fearing she had made a mistake in listening to the Duke and supposing she was making herself a laughing-stock not only to her own people but to his.

Then she realised that the alternative was so much more terrifying than the reality.

If she turned back now, she would be accepting her father's command to marry the dreaded Sir Ewen.

Anything, however terrifying, will surely be better than that.

The carriage slowed down.

As it turned in at the huge gates with a lodge on either side of them, it came to a standstill.

For a moment Sheinna wondered why.

Then the door of the carriage opened and the Duke himself stepped in.

He was smiling and she thought how handsome he looked as he pulled off his Highland bonnet and shook her hand.

"You are punctual," he declared, "which is what I expected. Let me tell you, Sheinna, you look marvellous."

"I was worried you might think I am overdressed," Sheinna replied in a small voice.

"This is an exciting adventure and I was half afraid you would not come at the last moment."

"How could I when I had given you my word?"

The Duke smiled.

"Very easily, where most women are concerned! Is it not a woman's privilege to say 'yes' when she means 'no' – and 'no' when she means 'yes'?"

Sheinna laughed.

"You must have met some very strange women. They cannot have belonged to the right Clan!"

"That is exactly what I thought, but now that we are going into battle together who could possibly defeat us?"

Sheinna gave a little shiver.

"You are so brave," she said, "but I am frightened. I know Papa will be absolutely furious. He has gone this morning to see the Minister of the Kirk."

"About your wedding?" the Duke asked her. "He is certainly wasting no time."

"Suppose you cannot save me, Your Grace?"

"Now don't you be afraid, Sheinna, I promised you that I would save you and that is what I will do, as well as saving myself. Just pick up your chin and tell yourself that we are invincible and no one can beat us!"

"I do hope you are right," she sighed anxiously.

The carriage was now moving more slowly and she realised that the horses were wheeling around so that they could alight at the porticoed front door.

The Castle soared high above them and Sheinna could now see that it was even more beautiful than she had thought it was when she had seen it years ago.

A footman opened the door and she stepped out of the carriage followed by the Duke.

He took her arm and helped her up the steps and in through the front door.

As he did so he exclaimed,

"Welcome to Barenlock Castle, Sheinna, and I will enjoy showing you my ancestral home!"

"It is something I have always wanted to see."

"Now, please don't call me 'Your Grace' anymore. It is far too formal especially as we are to be engaged – my name is Alpin."

"Yes, Your – I mean Alpin."

They were in the hall and she thought the butler and footmen were regarding her curiously.

The Duke held out his hand.

"Let me help you up the stairs," he offered. "My mother will be in the drawing room and with her will be my cousin, the Countess of Dunkeld.

"Oh, I have heard about her. She is very smart and is always written about in the newspapers."

The Duke smiled.

"That sounds exactly like my cousin Moira. Don't be frightened of her. She is one of those people who are determined I should be married. Not of course to someone of my choice – but of hers!"

He spoke rather bitterly and Sheinna looked at him in surprise.

They had now reached the landing.

A footman in attendance there opened the door into the drawing room.

Sheinna drew in her breath sharply and so did the Duke although she did not notice it.

As they walked in, the Duke's mother, the Dowager Duchess, who was sitting by the window, looked round.

So did the Countess who was sitting beside her.

"Mama," the Duke began, "I have brought you a big surprise and someone I particularly want you to meet."

The Dowager Duchess was looking questioningly at Sheinna.

"Of course, dearest," she replied. "Any friend of yours is always very welcome."

"I really hoped you would say that, Mama, because Sheinna MacFallin has just paid me the great honour of promising to be my wife."

For a moment there was complete silence.

Then as the Dowager Duchess gasped, the Countess cried,

"*MacFallin*! You surely cannot be a member of the MacFallin Clan which marches beside us."

The Dowager Duchess with great difficulty forced herself to say,

"This is a great surprise – Alpin, dear."

"I knew it would be, Mama, but Sheinna and I have known each other for some time. And we have decided to announce our engagement, even though we do not intend to be married for quite a while."

His mother, who had shaken Sheinna by the hand was apparently, for the moment, tongue-tied.

The Duke turned towards his cousin.

"And this," he added, "is my cousin, the Countess of Dunkeld."

Sheinna put out her hand.

The Countess took it and at the same time she said,

"I did not realise, Alpin, that you knew any of the MacFallin Clan. Perhaps she is not a near relation of our neighbour who behaves so badly and who we have always disliked."

"I am afraid," Sheinna now piped up, "that is my father."

"Your father!" the Countess exclaimed. "Then of course it is impossible for you and Alpin to be married."

"I think, Cousin Moira, that is for *me* to say," the Duke came in firmly. "I would be very sorry if you tried to pick a quarrel with someone who will be my wife."

For a moment the Countess could not think of a sharp reply.

The Dowager Duchess said quickly,

"Suppose you sit down, dearest Alpin, and tell me why you have kept this a secret until now. I had no idea, absolutely none, that you ever had any contact with the MacFallins."

Before the Duke could answer her, she turned to Sheinna,

"You must forgive me, my dear, if your appearance and my son's introduction have taken our breath away. We were talking only yesterday about him getting married, and he told us quite firmly he had no intention of marrying anyone."

"Then, naturally, you must be delighted that I am doing exactly what you have asked me to do," the Duke countered. "Sheinna and I are quite certain we will make an admirable bride and bridegroom."

"And what does your father say about all this?" the Countess asked Sheinna rather sharply.

The Duke thought it might be a somewhat difficult question for Sheinna to answer.

But very tactfully she replied,

"I think you must ask him that question yourself."

The Duke, who had not sat down when Sheinna did, put out his hand.

"Come and see the Castle," he invited her, "before you are asked any more questions. I find they are always a great bore."

"I would love to see the Castle," said Sheinna. "I have always admired it from the outside and thought it looked as if it had stepped straight out of a fairytale."

"That is exactly what it has done!"

He was leading her across the room as he spoke.

Only as the door shut behind them did the Dowager Duchess gasp,

"I don't believe it! However, she is pretty and very smartly dressed."

"Just how can he possibly marry a MacFallin?" the Countess asked angrily. "You know as well as I do that we have been at war with them for centuries. Her father, the Earl, is a horrible man. I have met him once or twice at parties and always thought he was someone I had no wish to meet again."

"I suppose Alpin must have known her for a long time," the Dowager Duchess added a little faintly.

"If that is so, he has been very wise to keep it to himself. Otherwise I would have had a lot to say on the matter," the Countess snapped.

"Oh, please don't be unkind to Alpin. You have bullied him into getting married, and now he is doing what you wanted, you will have to accept it even if the girl is a MacFallin."

"It is impossible, completely impossible for him to marry her," the Countess asserted. "You can imagine what all of our Clansmen will think. The Earl has always been abominably offensive and rude. He accused your husband of poaching his salmon and his game, and he is now doing the same to Alpin. How can you even speak to the man, let alone accept his daughter as Alpin's wife?"

"If he really loves her and wants to marry her," the Dowager Duchess said quietly, "then I will do my best for Alpin's sake to be fond of her and to help her."

She paused for a moment before continuing,

"I cannot help thinking it will be very difficult for her at home. If we McBarens are not ready to embrace the MacFallins, who loathe us with a deadly hatred, they will undoubtedly make trouble when they find out that Alpin is taking away the most precious member of their Clan after the Earl."

"It is something that just cannot happen," declared the Countess aggressively. "How can Alpin be so stupid as to choose her of all people? What has she to offer him except that small piece of land which should really belong to us?"

"I don't suppose she will inherit it. I believe she has two brothers, one of whom is in the Army and the other in Edinburgh – at least I think so."

"You cannot make it anything but a horrible and terrible mistake. I don't suppose she will have a penny of the Earl's money, if he has any, and Alpin cannot support a wife in his present state of affairs let alone restore the estate and the Castle as we all want him to do."

"I think, dear Moira, that although you mean well, you have pushed Alpin too hard. He always said he did not wish to get married until he fell in love with someone very special. While I do agree with you it is a misfortune that he wishes to marry a MacFallin, it may well turn out to be a blessing in disguise."

"I cannot think how it possibly can. As you are well aware, everyone in our Clan loathes the MacFallins, and they loathe us. It would be completely impossible for any marriage between our two families to be anything but a tragedy."

The Countess spoke angrily and, as if she found it impossible to contain her feelings, she stood up and walked across the room.

"Somehow," she then snapped, "although I am not certain how, we *have* to prevent it."

The Dowager Duchess gave a cry.

"No dear Moira, that would be a mistake. If Alpin wants her for his wife, then we must accept her and make the best of a bad job. Whatever happens we cannot, and I certainly will not, upset or hurt my son."

"You may feel like that," the Countess growled, "but I feel very differently. If you think I am going to accept that ghastly old Earl into my family, you are very much mistaken. I have to make Alpin see sense!"

"I beg you to leave him alone, Moira. I cannot help thinking, as I said before, that you have driven him to this because you have kept pushing him to marry Mary-Lee. I knew from the very beginning that he had no wish for his wife to be an American."

"What does it really matter who she is – with all that money?"

"Well, it matters to Alpin and now he has chosen someone he wants to marry, we have to make the very best of it."

She spoke bravely, but there was a note of despair in her voice.

As the Countess walked to the window in disgust, the Dowager Duchess wiped away a tear.

She was thinking that there was nothing they could do now except pray that by some miracle Alpin would be happy, even though his bride would be a MacFallin.

CHAPTER FIVE

The Duke showed Sheinna the view from the top of the Castle.

He pointed out especially the gardens and the place where he intended to build his museum. At the moment there was only a hut there containing the heads of lions he had killed in India, the first stag he had shot as a small boy and of course his first salmon.

There were also a number of unusual objects he had picked up in foreign parts and Sheinna longed to examine them all.

But he hurried her down again because he wanted to show her the other rooms and she was most impressed with them all.

He proudly showed her into the dining room with its large family portraits and then the library with all its old volumes of the history of Scotland and the Clans.

Finally he took her into his own study and, when she saw his travel books, she gave a cry of delight.

"There are so many about foreign countries".

"I know," the Duke replied. "They are about places I have visited and those I wish to visit. I try to learn about them, if possible, before I journey there."

"That is so sensible of you, Alpin. Otherwise you might miss something important."

"I thought that myself, but there are a number of books here on places I will never get a chance to see."

"Then I suppose we must be content with travelling in our minds," remarked Sheinna.

The Duke looked at her in surprise.

It was something no other woman had ever said to him.

"Do you really do that?" he enquired.

"You have been so lucky to have gone to some of these places, but I have only read about them and you must tell me much more than I know already."

"I would be delighted to and I will also show you the souvenirs I brought back. Some of them are small and just souvenirs, but others are more significant and when I look at them, I remember their background and the people I met in that particular country."

"If you can tell me about Nepal, India and most especially China, I will be living here for ever and you will never be able to get rid of me!"

As she spoke she looked over her shoulder just in case someone was at the door and she was being indiscreet.

"You are quite safe," said the Duke, "we cannot be overheard. At the same time be careful what you say when you are with others – "

A little later, as they were still talking in his study, Rory came in to give the Duke a message.

The Duke read it and then he asked.

"Is there a dinner party here tonight?"

"Oh, yes, Your Grace," replied Rory, "her Ladyship arranged it several days ago, then the visitors who came last night arrived rather unexpectedly, so we had dancing last night as well as tonight."

"I had no idea – "

He waited until Rory had left and then he turned to Sheinna,

"I think after all it would be a mistake for us to go and see your father this afternoon. I had no idea there is to be a party here tonight, but it would be a good idea for you to meet our friends who live in this part of the County."

"Yes – of course," Sheinna agreed hesitantly.

"So shall we postpone what will undoubtedly be an uncomfortable encounter with your father?"

"I am not going to argue about that," Sheinna said in a low voice, "but I cannot possibly stay for dinner as I have nothing to wear."

The Duke thought for a moment and suggested,

"Sit down and write a note to your father saying you have been asked to a party with friends and are staying the night with them. Don't mention any name and he will never think for one moment that you are with me at the McBaren Castle."

"No, he most certainly will not."

"Then write another note to your maid," the Duke continued. "Tell her to pack one of your best dresses for this evening and several other clothes in case tomorrow you stay longer than we at first planned."

"Are you sure we can do this – ?"

"I am quite sure, Sheinna. I will send Rory with the notes. He is discretion itself and, if I tell him you are in hiding, he will understand."

Sheinna smiled.

"I think we are getting deeper and deeper into this all the time," she murmured. "I just cannot imagine how it will end."

"But of course," the Duke chuckled, "we will live happily ever after. The only person who will really resent our happiness will be Sir Ewen."

"Do *not* mention that man," Sheinna begged. "It makes me tremble even to think of him."

"Then just enjoy yourself tonight, Sheinna. As you have already said, we are in a Fairy Palace and we must both forget that there are any goblins outside!"

Again Sheinna looked over her shoulder before she whispered,

"Your cousin, the Countess, obviously hates me."

"If she does, it really does not matter to you. She has always been an interfering woman, but my mother is very fond of her, and when I am away, Moira is at least someone for her to talk to."

"I can understand your mother missing you, Alpin, and I suppose it is natural she would want you to marry and settle down here so that she will have grandchildren to interest her."

"I will do that one day," the Duke said bitterly, "but as you understand, there is still a great deal of the world I wish to explore before I am shut up here, and have nothing more exciting to occupy me than the feud between your Clan and mine."

The way he spoke made Sheinna laugh.

She thought it would be exciting to be at a party tonight and the Duke was so right in saying that they might as well postpone the awful moment when she had to tell her father about their engagement.

She sat down at the writing table and the Duke gave her a piece of plain writing paper and a pen.

In her clear and elegant handwriting Sheinna told her father that she was staying away for a party tonight and she knew he would surely understand just how much she always looked forward to dancing the Scottish reels.

The Duke watching over her shoulder observed,

"That ought to pacify him. Now while I put this into an envelope for you, instuct your maid as to exactly what you need packed."

Sheinna made out a list and then closed the second envelope.

The Duke took the two letters to give them to Rory.

He did not ring the bell as he thought it would be embarrassing for Sheinna that he was ordering a servant to deceive her father.

"Please understand, Rory," he told the butler when he found him in the hall, "you are on no account to say who you are or where you come from."

Rory was listening intently.

"If you are asked where the party is taking place," the Duke went on, "or where her Ladyship is staying, you must just look vague."

"Please leave it to me, Your Grace," Rory asserted. "Your Grace knows I always enjoy a secret!"

The Duke knew this to be true.

When he was a boy, it was always Rory, who was a footman then, who would creep out with him at night and it was usually to swim in the sea or to spy on the poachers on the river.

It was Rory who would take him to the top of the moor where the snow was lying deep and when everyone else warned that it was too dangerous.

He realised that Rory would appreciate even better than anyone else what a commotion it would cause when he announced formally that he and Sheinna were engaged to be married.

He had not told him yet what they were planning, but he was certain for several good reasons that Rory had his suspicions of what was going on –

One was that his cousin, the Countess, as always had been talking so loud, and another, that a MacFallin had not crossed the threshold of the Castle for at least fifty years.

"I'll be as quick as I can, Your Grace," Rory said as the Duke handed him the notes. "As you'll be dancing the reels tonight, I'm having your best kilt pressed and your finest sporran taken out of the safe."

That particular ceremonial sporran had been worn by the Chieftain of the McBarrens for generations. It was a fine piece of workmanship and the fur on it was owed to the keen eye and good marksmanship of its first owner.

The Duke smiled.

He mused, if nothing else, he and Sheinna would enjoy an amusing evening before they went into battle.

'I don't want her to become upset or depressed,' he thought. 'While this idea of mine will save her from being forced to marry the ghastly Sir Ewen, there will undoubtedly be many unpleasant moments ahead for both of us.'

He walked back to the study to find that Sheinna was engrossed in a book on India she had taken down from one of the shelves.

"I have been looking at the illustrations and reading about the North-West Frontier," she sighed. "How I would love to go to India!"

"Perhaps it would be a good place to travel to if we have to run away?"

"Now you are not to try and make me believe that is possible, but it's a country that I would rather visit than anywhere else in the world."

"I thought that when I was out there, but I was even more fascinated by Nepal, perhaps because it is so close to the Himalayas."

"Tell me about them, please tell me about them," Sheinna begged him. "If I was a man, I would try to climb them, but as I am a woman I must be content to kneel at their feet and look up at them."

"They are just incredibly beautiful. I will find you other books which will tell you more about the Himalayas than the one you are reading."

"Oh, thank you, thank you, Alpin," she enthused. "I only hope that I will be able to absorb them before I am dragged away from you by Papa."

"We must prevent him from doing so – otherwise he will force you to marry Sir Ewen and you will then be unable to escape again."

He saw the expression of fear in her eyes and that she trembled.

He suggested quickly,

"Forget about him, we are going to enjoy ourselves tonight as if we were two people very much in love with each other and celebrating with our friends."

"You are not going to tell them we are engaged?" Sheinna asked him.

"I think we should do. It will be more difficult for your father to force you up the aisle with Sir Ewen or even to take you home as a prisoner if so many people know about our engagement."

He paused before he added,

"They will be just astonished, but it will give them something new to talk about."

"Are you quite certain that we are doing the right thing?" Sheinna asked him. "I am thinking of you and how it will be very very difficult for you, Alpin, when everyone is horrified at your intention to marry a MacFallin."

"I don't think everyone will be horrified. Many of the guests who are coming tonight, I should imagine, are quite unaware of the animosity between our two Clans."

Sheinna looked surprised, but he carried on,

"Some of them come from Edinburgh, others from London. I had really forgotten that my cousin was holding such a big party. It is in fact her daughter's birthday."

He remembered as he spoke that he had asked his mother to buy a present for him to give to the birthday girl and he only hoped she had not forgotten, as he had.

"If everyone is so interested in the birthday party," Sheinna commented, "they will not then be concentrating on us."

The Duke thought that this was wishful thinking, but he did not say so.

He could easily imagine the disagreeable comments his cousin Moira would make about the MacFallins.

Then he thought the one thing he should do was to keep Sheinna from being too worried about what might happen at the party.

He therefore talked about India until it was time to go and dress for dinner.

But before they did so he took Sheinna once again up to the top of the Castle to view the sunset.

The lights in that part of Scotland were known to be some of the most stunning ever and the sun was sinking slowly behind the hills, while its last rays illuminated the moors on either side of the bay.

It was far more glorious the Duke considered than anything one could experience in India or anywhere else in the world for that matter.

He sensed as they stood together in silence on the top of one of the towers that Sheinna felt the same.

When the sun vanished and they looked up, the first evening star was glittering overhead.

"Thank you, thank you, Alpin," Sheinna muttered. "This is something I will always remember. You are the luckiest man in the world to be able to stand on your own Castle and see anything so indescribably wonderful."

The way she spoke to him and the deep sincerity in her voice was, the Duke felt, very moving.

He was used to women who were only animated when he was talking about themselves and who had little enthusiasm for the world he loved and wanted to explore.

When they climbed down the narrow steps from the tower, Sheinna went to her bedroom.

She thought it was beautifully furnished and very luxurious, but she would have taken it for granted if she was still in England.

She had indeed not expected to find anything quite so comfortable in Scotland and when she compared it with her own home, she thought it was absurd for her father to be so behind the times.

He did not realise that people had progressed and in doing so they expected more for themselves than they had ever desired in the past.

She had always taken it for granted that the rich people in England would have fine houses in London and even larger and more prestigious ones in the country.

It was thus only since she had returned to Scotland that she had realised how out-of-date and uncomfortable her home was.

Here in the Castle everything was in perfect good taste and no visitor could find fault with anything.

Her clothes that Rory brought back from her home were already unpacked and hanging in the wardrobe and a bath was arranged on the hearth in front of the fire.

There was a small fire burning in the grate as, when the sun went down, a cold wind blew in from the sea.

Her four-poster bed was draped with copious velvet curtains and there were several mirrors in which she could see her own reflection.

"You have plenty of time," the Duke told her as he showed her into the room. "I have learnt that the guests are arriving for dinner at eight o'clock."

"Where shall I go – when I am ready?" she asked in a frightened voice.

"We will meet in the large drawing room, which is a little further along the corridor where you met my mother earlier. There will be a footman outside to open the door for you. I promise I will be there, so that you will not have to enter the room alone."

"Oh, thank you!" Sheinna exclaimed. "I shall be very shy because I expect I will know no one."

"You will know me," the Duke replied, "and I will look after you this evening, Sheinna. So don't be afraid."

She smiled at him.

He thought that unlike many women he had known she was not demanding or clinging to him.

He went to his own room to find that his valet was waiting for him with his bath.

By the time he had changed he realised that it was only twenty minutes to eight and it would be a kindness to Sheinna if he picked her up before she left her bedroom.

He could understand too well that she would be shy in walking into a room where she knew no one – except for his mother and his cousin Moira, who he was sure would continue being hostile.

He knocked on Sheinna's door and a maid opened it.

"I came to see if her Ladyship is ready."

Before the maid could answer Sheinna ran across the room to him.

"I was waiting in here," she breathed, "just in case you were not in the drawing room when I went there."

"Come along, we will brave them together and let me tell you that you look very lovely, Sheinna."

He was not exaggerating.

She was wearing a beautiful gown she had bought in Paris, which had been designed by the famous Frederick Worth, the greatest modern *couturier* of the fashion world.

The gown was suprimely elegant and at the same time it enhanced the graceful curves of her figure.

It was a soft shade of blue, which was a perfect frame for her translucent skin and glorious fair hair with its touch of fire.

One glance told the Duke that she would astound anyone who lived locally and even outclass anyone who came from London.

As they went into the passage, Sheinna commented,

"Now I can understand why the Scots wear the kilt. No gentleman could look smarter than you do. If there are any Englishmen here tonight, they will indeed have to look to their laurels!"

"Thank you. Now, as we are both so pleased with one another, we will make a dramatic entrance!"

Sheinna thought she would really prefer to creep in unnoticed, but it would be rude to argue with her host.

She therefore merely trembled a little.

The piper standing in the passage was asked to play the stirring tune of the *McBarens' Salute to the Chieftain* and, as he did so, the Duke told the footman to throw open the doors.

The Duke offered Sheinna his arm.

There were already about twenty-five people in the large drawing room. Most were young and only the older gentlemen were wearing the kilt. The girls were dressed in their very best evening gowns, but they did not even begin to compare with Sheinna's.

There was a cry of delight as the Duke appeared.

Then he started to shake hands with the guests and to introduce Sheinna as his fiancée.

Most of them thought it very exciting that he was engaged to be married, but did not understand that there was anything at all peculiar about his engagement.

Sheinna, however, was aware that the Countess was scowling.

She thought it particularly tactful of the Duke when he deliberately ignored his cousin and stayed amongst the younger guests.

He was talking and laughing with them and telling them that Sheinna had recently come North from London.

As most of them were from other parts of Scotland and had no idea of the feud between the McBarens and the MacFallins, they talked to Sheinna as if she was one of them.

When they went into dinner, the Duke had altered the *placement* at the table with Rory, having thrown away the original plan that had been arranged by his mother and his cousin.

Tonight all the youngsters were at his end of the table, while the older generation were at the other end.

Sheinna sat on his right and a pretty girl, who he had met before, was on his left.

The dinner was delicious and the party were all laughing and talking as if nothing unusual had occurred –

with, of course, the exception of the Countess who was looking daggers at the Duke all through the meal. She had made no effort to speak either to him or to Sheinna.

When dinner was finished and the piper had piped around the table, the Duke led the way to the Chieftain's room on the ground floor.

All the walls were covered with the horned heads of stags.

Tonight there was not just a single pianist but a small band already playing when they entered the room.

They started off with Scottish reels.

The Duke had expected that, as Sheinna had been living with her grandmother in London, she would not be able to take part in them, but to his surprise she danced them better and more gracefully than anyone else.

He was of course her partner and when they could speak, he exclaimed,

"I had no idea you were so good at all the reels."

"I loved them when I was a child," said Sheinna. "When I was in London I had a number of Scottish friends, so we kept ourselves in practice."

"You dance them far better than anyone I have ever seen."

"Now you are flattering me, Alpin. May I say that you are very good yourself."

"I have to be. A Chieftain who could not dance the reels would be deposed immediately!"

Sheinna laughed.

"That will never happen to you and I am enjoying having you as my partner. In fact you are as good on the dance floor as you are on the river."

"Now that is the sort of compliment I like to hear!"

Now they both laughed.

In fact they were laughing happily all the evening.

When the band struck up a dreamy waltz, the Duke found that Sheinna danced as well as anyone he had ever had as his partner.

"Why did I not meet you in London?" he asked as they moved smoothly around the room.

"I can answer that question quite easily," Sheinna replied. "You were far too busy, Alpin, enjoying yourself at Marlborough House and ignoring, where possible, the dances given for *debutantes*."

This was true.

The Duke remembered how he had avoided those dances simply because he was an undeniable matrimonial catch.

"I never thought," Sheinna was saying softly, "that I would be privileged to dance like this in Scotland or in any house as magnificent and majestic as your Castle."

The Duke swung her round without answering.

He was thinking that they were certainly a perfect match on the dance floor.

As far as Sheinna was concerned the dancing came to an end far too quickly.

Some of the guests had to drive a long way home and so in the early hours of the morning they said sadly that they must leave.

All of them had brought a present for Charlotte's birthday and they were arranged on a table near the door.

Charlotte stood with Mary-Lee beside her thanking everyone for all her presents and begging those who lived nearer not to go home so soon.

They had drunk Charlotte's health at dinner and there had been a special birthday cake for her.

Charlotte was pretty in her own special way, the Duke thought, but if he compared her with Sheinna, she looked very countrified and somewhat heavily built.

There was little doubt that she had greatly enjoyed her birthday ball and the young gentlemen had fought with each other to dance with her.

The Duke, however, made no effort to dance with anyone except Sheinna and since the guests had been told they were engaged, that was what they expected.

At the same time he was aware that Mary-Lee was looking at him almost pleadingly.

"I hope you have enjoyed the evening, Mary-Lee," he enquired.

"It has been real wonderful," she replied, "except you haven't danced with me."

The Duke smiled.

"I felt you would understand that since my fiancée knows very few people here and I don't want any man to take my place, I have found it difficult to be as pleasant as I wanted to be to you and the other charming young ladies present."

"Please dance with me now," Mary-Lee asked. "I do want to boast when I go back home to the States that I have danced with a real Scottish Duke. Last night you did not come into the room where we were dancing."

The Duke looked round quickly.

Then he saw one of his friends with whom he had often stayed standing without a partner but with a glass of champagne in his hand.

"We will dance the next dance, Mary-Lee," he said "if you will just wait for me to introduce Charles Faulkner to Sheinna."

"You can be certain I'll wait right here," Mary-Lee replied, speaking in her broad American accent.

The Duke took Sheinna across to Charles Faulkner.

"I have rather neglected my guests who are staying in the Castle," he said, "so would you be kind, Charles, and look after my fiancée for a few minutes?"

"When I heard you were engaged to be married," Charles Faulkner replied, "I did not believe it, Alpin."

"Well, it is true and I will talk to you later. Now please look after Lady Sheinna and don't allow anyone to upset her."

"I will do so," Charles answered, "but unfortunately I did not bring my *skean dhu* with me!"

Sheinna smiled.

"I know what that is and if you were not dancing you would be wearing it in your stocking."

"And most uncomfortable it would feel," Charles added. "Can I fetch you a drink, Sheinna?"

"I would just love a glass of lemonade."

He did not persuade her to have champagne which he was drinking and he took a glass of lemonade from a footman standing by the door with a tray of glasses.

They sat down when the dance started and the Duke led Mary-Lee onto the floor

Then Charles asked Sheinna,

"Is it really true you are engaged to Alpin?"

She nodded.

"Yes, but he told his mother only today."

"And what does your father say about it?" Charles enquired. "I have always understood that he loathes and detests all the McBarens. People laugh at the way he is so vehement against my friend Alpin."

"Perhaps in some way we will be able to put an end to the ridiculous feud between our families. After all we both live in and love this beautiful part of Scotland and it is silly for us to go on fighting for no particular reason except that we always did so in the past."

"I agree with you absolutely," replied Charles. "I am a Scot, but I live on the border and thank goodness we have given up our feuds there including even our hatred of the English."

"I have found a great number of Englishmen very charming," said Sheinna.

"I am sure they feel the same about you – "

There was silence for a moment, then he went on,

"So if you and Alpin could bring your Clansmen together and make them forget the way they have hated each other all down the centuries, I think it would be a great moment for Scotland and a step forward for everyone who lives here."

"You are repeating exactly what I have been saying myself. Please will you help Alpin? It's very difficult for him when his own relations hate my father and his people."

She glanced across the room at the Countess.

Charles Faulkner knew exactly what she was saying and lowering his voice, he confided,

"The Countess is one of the older generation who will never change their ways, but the younger ones, who like yourself are growing up, think this animosity between the Clans is old-fashioned and out of date."

"So do I," Sheinna asserted.

"After all, we are all Scots," Charles added, "and that we are of the same blood should matter more than anything else."

"That is exactly what I feel. Please, please go on saying it."

"I will," Charles agreed. "As I shoot and fish here with Alpin every year, I should be honoured if your father would ask me to be his guest."

Sheinna managed a smile.

Although she thought it was very unlikely, she said,

"I am sure that my father would be delighted to welcome you."

"I will greatly look forward to you asking me. I have always been a guest at Alpin's first shoot and I would be hurt and upset if I could not be his guest this year as well."

"If you were indeed forgotten, would you blame me?" Sheinna asked Charles.

"I cannot believe that you would be so unkind. In fact I should cry my eyes out, as this shoot is one of my best invitations during the whole year."

"I will make sure you are not forgotten, Charles."

As she spoke she was wondering if she would still be with the Duke when the autumn came.

One thing she was quite sure of – if her father knew Charles Faulkner was Alpin's friend, he would definitely *not* be a guest on their moors.

The Duke, having danced with Mary-Lee for nearly ten minutes, came back to her side.

"Has Charles looked after you?" he enquired.

"He has been very attentive," Sheinna replied. "We have both decided that the animosity and hatred between the Clans is ridiculous and should be banned once and for all."

"I believe that it will be gradually," said the Duke. "Perhaps you and I, Sheinna, will make a great number of people on either side of our two families realise that we are not as hateful as they thought we were."

"I only hope you are right," she sighed.

She was thinking as she spoke that she would never be welcomed with open arms by the Countess, nor would the Duke ever cross the threshold of her father's house.

As if the Duke sensed what she was thinking and could read her thoughts, he declared,

"You are so right, Sheinna, and somehow you and I will make them both accept the flag of peace."

"Of course," Charles came in, "that is what we all want, peace and prosperity, and it is something I am quite prepared to fight for."

"No fighting allowed," the Duke stipulated firmly. "What we must do is to appeal to the hearts of our people and make them realise that whatever name they are called, whatever blood they bear, it is they themselves who can make Scotland a happy or an unhappy place."

"I will join your crusade," Charles exclaimed. "Put me down as a flag-bearer or would you rather I played the pipes?"

"I will make you do both," the Duke chuckled, "and what you have to do now, Charles, is to persuade a great number of others to think as you and I do."

"We can certainly try, Alpin, and what could be better than that you and this beautiful girl should marry each other and set an example to all the Clans in Scotland."

"You are making our marriage seem even more important than I knew it was for me!"

"I think it will be very important for us all," replied Charles. "It is time this part of Scotland moved with the times and you stopped fighting amongst yourselves. I have a feeling that our enemies are much further away."

He paused before he added,

"I may be wrong, but time will show us eventually where our real foes will come from. I am convinced it will be from Europe."

"I sincerely hope you are wrong," said the Duke.

He was about to say more, but several guests came up to bid him goodnight and knowing of his engagement they wished him every possible happiness and the same to Sheinna.

It was only when the last guest had departed that Sheinna enthused to the Duke,

"That was a wonderful party and I did enjoy it."

"I am very glad. Needless to say you were a great success. Everybody told me they thought that you were incredibly beautiful and no one will ever dispute that!"

They were walking together towards the door as he was speaking.

Then, as they turned to ascend the stairs, they heard the voice of the Countess saying to the Dowager Duchess,

"It has been a marvellous evening and Charlotte has never had a better birthday. In fact there was only one blot on the horizon and you know without my telling you what that was!"

There was a harsh note in her voice.

Without even meaning to, Sheinna drew just a little closer to the Duke and slipped her hand into his.

His fingers closed over hers.

"Don't listen," he urged quietly. "Tonight we have started our crusade and we must expect some opposition. But sooner or later – and this is a prophecy – all the people will join us and Scotland will be a whole country and not a divided one."

"I will pray it will come true," Sheinna murmured.

"I guessed you would," answered the Duke.

CHAPTER SIX

The next morning when Sheinna came downstairs to breakfast, it was to find the Duke was already there, but there was no sign of anyone else.

"The rest of the guests are still sleeping," the Duke greeted her, "and I did not expect you to be up so early."

"I enjoyed myself so much last night that I was not even tired."

The Duke smiled.

"You certainly danced all the reels much better than anyone else and indeed far, far better than I expected."

"I do love dancing."

"So do I at times, but naturally it depends who I am dancing with!"

Sheinna laughed.

"I am sure you had an extensive choice in London. My grandmother told me that all the great beauties go to Marlborough House."

The Duke did not reply and Sheinna thought that perhaps she had said too much and lapsed into silence.

But because she was curious she could not prevent herself asking,

"What are we going to do today?"

She was half afraid, as she asked the question, that the Duke would say he was taking her back to her father.

Instead he replied,

"I am thinking of something that will really interest you. I thought perhaps a short trip along the coast in my yacht would be exhilarating."

Sheinna gave a cry of delight.

"That will be wonderful. I would so much rather do that than anything else."

"I thought that you would, Sheinna. As it is a new yacht and I am very proud of it, I will probably talk about it incessantly."

"You could not talk too much for me, Alpin. I have never been on a yacht, but I have read so much about them, especially the clippers that are now being built in America. I always hoped someone would invite me on one."

"Well, that's settled then, but as I have some letters I must write and also, although it sounds very depressing, a large number of bills to settle, we will have to wait until later."

"Then I will go into the garden. The sun is shining and I want to admire the lovely blooms you have growing there."

"If you praise the gardeners they will be delighted," said the Duke. "They have taken a great deal of trouble while I have been away to make new beds and I am thrilled with the way they have come on so well."

"I had no idea you were interested in gardens?"

"Well, I am, and there is so much we have to learn about each other."

He glanced over his shoulder before he added,

"Otherwise they will guess we have only just met, and not known each other, as we pretended we had, for many years."

Sheinna laughed.

"I wish I had known you for many years. It would have been such fun to have met you in London."

Before the Duke could reply she went on,

"But I am sure you would have been far too busy to talk to me, because I was only a silly little *debutante*. My grandmother told me over and over again that the most intelligent gentlemen consider *debutantes* a bore."

The Duke laughed.

"That is true, but I would never have said you were a bore. In fact you have not bored me once since I have known you."

"But you can hardly say it's a very long time," she replied in a whisper.

"Some people I meet over and over again, yet I feel I never know any more about them than I did the first day I said, 'how do you do'. But others, like you, I feel I have known for ever and I am aware not only of what they are saying but what they are thinking."

Sheinna clapped her hands together.

"Oh, I am so glad you think like that. I have often felt like that myself and I know it's because in some cases we have met in other lives."

"Are you telling me," the Duke asked slowly, "that you believe in the *Wheel of Rebirth*?"

"Of course I do," she replied. "I could not have read all those books about the East without knowing that their philosophy is the only sensible reason for the world to exist."

She saw that the Duke was listening intently and went on,

"How could anyone with brilliant brains like Lord Melbourne and the Duke of Wellington just disappear and be forgotten except in print? Of course either they will live again in the Third Dimension or are advanced enough to go on to the Fourth."

The Duke looked at her in amazement and sat down again at the breakfast table.

"I am fascinated by what you are saying, Sheinna. It is what I learnt in the East and had never thought of it before. I have never found anyone who is as interested in the subject as I am."

"I feel the same. It is very exciting now to know that you and I are thinking on the same wavelength. You can help me puzzle out esoteric issues I don't understand."

"We can certainly try. When we are on my yacht this afternoon, we will not be disturbed, so we can really get down to brass tacks."

Sheinna laughed.

"That is hardly the right word for it, but I do know exactly what you mean and it will be very stimulating for me."

"And for me too," the Duke concurred.

He rose and walked towards the door.

"When I have finished my letters – and the bills – I will come and join you."

"You will find me in the garden as I have already told you, Alpin."

He smiled as he left the breakfast room, closing the door quietly behind him.

As she finished her coffee Sheinna thought this was the most exciting thing that had ever happened to her.

She had longed for someone to explain what was referred to in every book she had read about the East, but the young men whom she had danced with and talked to in London had either not travelled much or were uninterested.

Here, where she had least expected it, was someone who had really explored strange and unusual places and at the same time had been interested in the lives and religions of those who lived in them.

When she left the breakfast room, she did not go upstairs to put on her hat.

The sun was surely not too hot to burn her face and because she had lived so long in towns she liked the feeling of freedom and vitality in the Scottish air.

As she walked down the stone steps, she thought that the garden with its beautiful flowers and the butterflies and bees fluttering around them was something one could never find in a town.

There was nowhere more attractive than Scotland.

*

The Duke went to his study where there was a pile of letters left by his secretary, all requiring answers.

And there was a large bundle of bills to which were attached cheques.

He looked first at the letters, finding among them several from the ladies in London he had spent a great deal of his time with – they were all married and many of them boasted distinguished titles.

The letters they wrote to him were naturally very confidential and they had therefore not been opened by his secretary.

He had instructed them to print the word '*private*' on the envelope of any letter they wrote to him and then no one but he would open it.

However, he was in a hurry this morning.

He wanted to be with Sheinna, so he just pushed the letters marked 'private' on one side and opened only the others.

Some of them were from hostesses whose parties he had enjoyed and several were from his friends who had missed him in White's Club.

He noted as he read them that they hoped later on in the Season they would be invited to the Castle to shoot or fish.

He answered three letters and was just about to start signing the cheques when Rory came hurrying in.

"The Earl of MacFallin has just arrived to see you, Your Grace," he announced.

The Duke drew in his breath.

"*The Earl?*"

"Yes, Your Grace, and he's brought a number of his elders with him. I understand there be other members of the Clan outside as well."

The Duke was silent.

He was thinking that he had not anticipated this eventuality, although it was not altogether surprising.

"Where have you put his Lordship?" he asked.

"As there be that many of them, Your Grace, I have showed them into the Chieftain's Room and the footmen be arranging chairs for them."

The Duke rose from his writing desk.

"You said, Rory, that there were others of the Clan outside. I hope they are not here to make trouble."

"I hopes not, Your Grace, but I've sent one of the footmen to tell our own lads to be on guard."

The Duke smiled.

It was so like Rory to think that necessary.

Equally he had no wish for the Castle windows to be broken or a vulgar riot in his own grounds.

It would be a mistake, he felt, to disturb Sheinna by telling her that her father was here.

Instead he walked slowly towards the Chieftain's Room.

It had been a place of immense pleasure last night for the dancing and he thought it was typical that today it could well turn into more or less a Clan battleground.

He entered the room unattended.

He was aware as he did so that the Earl, looking extremely aggressive, was standing at the far end.

There were at least twenty elders seated behind him and about the same number of other members of the Clan standing.

As the Duke walked with dignity towards the Earl, he thought he looked very much older than he remembered him – but exceedingly disagreeable.

As he reached him neither of them made any effort to shake hands.

The Duke said quietly before the Earl could speak,

"Good morning, MacFallin. I understand that you wish to see me."

"Of course I want to see you," the Earl roared. "It has been rumoured, although I can hardly believe it is true, that you have had the audacity to announce that you intend to marry my daughter."

"Your daughter has paid me the great honour of promising to be my wife," the Duke replied seriously.

For a brief moment there was silence and then there came an audible murmur from the elders.

"*She will marry you over my dead body!*" the Earl shouted furiously. "Just how dare you get to know my daughter, as I imagine you did in London, and ask her to marry you when you have consistantly abused and insulted the MacFallins ever since you were born!"

"As you know," the Duke responded to this rant, "the hostility between our two Clans has lasted for at least four hundred years. I think it is high time we woke up to modern ideas and modern thinking and behaved sensibly."

"Are you saying I am not sensible?" the Earl asked, screaming the words at him.

"On the contrary, I feel sure you will be sensible enough to realise that in this century and in this time in our history we should all unite. If we must fight, let's fight for Scotland and not amongst ourselves!"

He sensed as he spoke the words there was almost a murmur of approval from the elders.

But the Earl flashed back,

"That may well be *your* idea, but it is certainly not *mine*."

"I don't see why not," the Duke persisted.

"As you might be well aware," the Earl yelled, "the MacFallins have fought for our country against the English and distinguished themselves at the Battle of Culloden, which is more than the cowardly McBarens did."

The Duke wanted to contradict him, but thought it would be unwise at this stage.

Instead he replied quietly,

"I was actually, my Lord, intending to call on you this afternoon to inform you of my engagement to your daughter, and to discuss how we can together contrive to make this part of Scotland much more prosperous than it is at present."

"Do you really think that I would listen to you?" the Earl howled furiously. "I hate and despise you, as all my life I have always hated the McBarens. I would rather see my daughter in the grave than married to you or any of your dissolute kin."

Because he was so violent there was a muttering of protest from the elders behind him and those standing in the hall looked at each other with some concern.

"What I am suggesting," said the Duke, "is that we sit down comfortably and talk over how we can help unite our Clans, as your daughter and I intend to do by being married."

The Earl's face went red with fury.

"If you think I would ever allow you to marry my daughter, then you are very much mistaken. She is already pledged to marry a friend of mine and I will take care that the marriage takes place as quickly as possible!"

He was shouting out the words wildly and his men looked at him in surprise.

"If you are thinking of marrying Sheinna off to Sir Ewen Kiscard, you must be mad," the Duke said sharply. "He is quite old enough to be her grandfather and has a reputation which stinks. No good father would entrust his young daughter to such a man. I can only beg you to see sense and if she cannot marry me at least she need not be sacrificed to your own perverse aggrandisement."

"How dare you speak to me in such a manner?" the Earl shouted. "Sheinna is my daughter and she will do as she is told. I have chosen a husband for her and they will be married as soon as I get them in front of the Minister."

He paused for breath before raging on,

"You keep your Clan and your own friends, most of whom I understand come from England, and leave us Scots to live our lives as we want!"

"I really think, my Lord, you are being somewhat unreasonable. Surely your daughter's wishes with regard to a husband are more important than anything else."

There were further mutterings from the elders as the Duke continued,

"No girl of her age would wish to be married to a man of seventy, who has dragged his name and his title through the gutter in a dozen different ways."

"As I have told you already," the Earl screamed, "Sheinna will marry whoever I shall wish her to marry. Sir

Ewen is already distressed, as he told me this morning, to hear that she is contemplating marrying someone like *you*."

Before the Duke could reply, he continued,

"You spend your time and your money in England instead of spending it here. You have allowed the poachers on your rivers to steal the salmon which should be coming up to mine. And from all I hear, this Castle, of which you are so proud, is falling down round your ears. I will make certain than no MacFallin helps you to put it to rights."

He was speaking so ferociously that he was almost foaming at the mouth.

The Duke was wondering what he could now say to calm him down.

Suddenly the door opened and Rory came running in and because he was moving so fast, the Duke turned to look at him in astonishment.

Everyone fell silent.

"Your Grace," Rory blurted out, "her Ladyship's been taken away."

"Taken away!" the Duke exclaimed. "What do you mean, Rory?"

"Some men," he gasped, "led by Sir Ewen Kiscard, carried her away out of the garden. Although her Ladyship were a-struggling, they puts her in a carriage with him and they drive off."

"I cannot believe it!"

"It be true, Your Grace, and them as seen her go says she was crying out for Your Grace."

The Duke turned to the Earl.

"Is this your doing?" he demanded sternly.

"No! No! I intend to take Sheinna home with me," the Earl replied weakly.

"Then why has Sir Ewen kidnapped her?" the Duke asked angrily. "There seems to be no other word for it."

"I really have no idea," the Earl stuttered. "But I expect he was determined she should not marry you and has therefore carried her away to make quite certain that she marries him."

"I have never heard of anything so outrageous," the Duke snorted. "I suggest that you and I follow them at once and prevent Sir Ewen from terrifying Sheinna, let alone marrying her. It is utterly monstrous that he should have abducted her out of my garden."

There was a murmur from the elders and the other Clansmen as if they agreed with him.

The Duke said quickly,

"There is no time to be lost. Come along, my Lord, we will follow them and if your horses are fast, we will overtake them. As you well know, your daughter will be exceedingly frightened by now and I am horrified that Sir Ewen should behave in such a criminal manner."

He was walking to the door as he spoke.

As if he could not bring himself to reply, the Earl followed him meekly and so did the Clansmen, while the elders began to rise from their chairs.

Without speaking, the Duke, with Rory leading the way, ran from the Chieftain's Room into the hall.

Directly outside the door was the carriage that had brought the Earl to the Castle and behind it were a number of other carriages and wagons that had conveyed the other members of the Clan.

Standing by the Duke's own carriage were two of his men who had seen Sheinna carried away.

"She was pickin' some flowers, Your Grace," one of them said, "when two men seized her up in their arms and runs off with her out of the garden and up them steps to where Sir Ewen were a-waitin'.""

"Was there no one to stop them?" the Duke asked.

"We be at the other end of the garden, Your Grace, when we hears a scream and runs to help her, but we was too late. We sees Sir Ewen in the carriage as they flings her beside him. Then they slams the door and drives off."

"How many men were with him?"

"Only four, Your Grace, and the man drivin' the carriage."

"Which way did they go?"

"We expected them to go left, but I sees them after they went through the gates, passin' down the cliff road towards the village."

The Duke knew that at the village the river ran into the sea and there was a small harbour in which there were usually a number of small fishing boats.

If Sir Ewen had gone there, he might be intending to take Sheinna away by sea and it would be very difficult to find her again.

Turning to Rory he ordered,

"Follow me with my carriage and as many of our men as you can muster."

He then climbed into the Earl's carriage, which was in front of all the others, and snapped,

"Move as quickly as you can. We have to reach the village before Sir Ewen does."

There were two horses drawing the carriage, which was certainly not as comfortable as his own nor were the horses as fast.

The Duke's only hope as they moved up the drive was that perhaps Sir Ewen's horses were rough – not in any way as well bred as those he owned or the Earl's.

The Duke became aware that two of his men had jumped up at the back of the carriage and there were two on the box beside the driver.

As he looked back he could see the other carriages, which had brought the MacFallin elders and the Clansmen to the Castle, were now following them.

They turned right after passing through the gates.

There was a straight road running along the side of the river and it was, as the Duke knew, about two miles to the village.

The Earl was muttering to himself, but he did not say anything aloud.

The Duke guessed he was exceedingly annoyed at his friend Sir Ewen for interfering in his business.

They drove in silence, the driver doing his best to move his horses as quickly as he could.

But there was no sign anywhere of Sir Ewen on the road ahead.

Then a little further on, the moors rose on the left hand side of the road and on the right were fields in which lambs were grazing between the road and the river.

They were more than a mile from the village when the Duke gave a loud exclamation.

Even as he did so the men sitting on the box of the carriage pointed with their hands.

There was a piece of waste land on their left and it was rough moorland the Duke knew only too well.

When the Vikings raided Scotland, they found this particular part of the country was low-lying and easy to invade, so the villagers and Clansmen at that time had built a hiding place for themselves.

They had dug into the hillside and at the end of quite a long tunnel they had excavated a large cave. In it they could hide themselves, their children and even a good number of their animals.

When there were no longer any Viking invasions, the children in the village found it an amusing place to play in, and of course, there were sightseers too.

Later a Duke learnt it was in a dangerous condition and it was reported to His Grace that because the soil there was sandy the roof of the cave was already collapsing.

And it was only a question of time before the tunnel which led to it would also fall in.

In which case anyone inside might be buried alive and the then Duke therefore had the entrance boarded up.

He had given orders that no one was to go into what was known locally as 'the Vikings hiding-place'.

Now, to the present Duke's utter astonishment, Sir Ewen's carriage, which bore his crest, was standing beside the entrance to the tunnel.

"If that is where Sir Ewen has taken Sheinna," he cried angrily, speaking for the first time since they left the Castle, "there is every likelihood she will be buried alive!"

"I'll kill that man for interfering," the Earl growled.

"Let's get Sheinna to safety first," the Duke said. "She is more important than anyone else."

As if the Earl felt he could not argue about that, he was silent.

The Earl's carriage then turned off the road and it moved rather rockily across the ground towards Sir Ewen's carriage.

Even as the horses came to a standstill, four men appeared out of the tunnel.

They saw that the Earl was approaching and that there was a string of carriages behind him, so they threw down the tools they were carrying and fled up the moor above the tunnel.

The Earl jumped out almost nimbly for a man of his age and hurried across the rough ground towards Sir Ewen.

He had almost reached him with the Duke close behind, when to his complete amazement Sir Ewen, who looked even more unpleasant than he recalled, shouted,

"If I cannot have her, no one else shall!"

Somewhat breathlessly the Earl snapped at him,

"Where have you taken my daughter? How dare you interfere, I told you I would deal with the Duke and you were to wait for me to bring her back."

By this time the Duke was standing beside the Earl and the McBaren Clansmen who had come with them in their carriages were only a yard or so away.

In fact some from another carriage were coming up behind Sir Ewen.

"Get out of my way!" the Earl shouted. "I will not have my daughter carried off by you or anyone else."

As he spat out the last words, he looked towards the Duke and as he did so, Sir Ewen raised his hand in which he was holding a small pistol and shot at the Earl.

The bullet grazed the top of the Earl's scalp and, as he fell backwards, he gave a shriek of agony.

For a moment the Duke was so dumbfounded he could not move.

Then one of his Clansmen who had approached Sir Ewen from behind struck him violently with a heavy stick.

He too fell over, dropping his pistol and sprawling on the ground.

The Duke ran to the opening of the tunnel.

As he did so he saw an oil lamp lying on the ground

that had obviously been used by Sir Ewen's men when they carried Sheinna in.

He picked it up, saw it was still burning and looked round. Behind him were two of his own men and several others who had followed in his carriage.

"See that no one follows me. It's very dangerous," he called out sharply and disappeared into the tunnel.

He had been there as a boy many years ago.

He now saw that there was a great deal of sand on the ground and he thought, although he could not be sure, that the roof overhead had partially collapsed.

The opening, however, was still just wide enough to have allowed sufficient room for the two men to carry Sheinna in.

The Duke now pressed on as quickly as he could towards the 'Vikings hiding-place'.

He reached the end of the tunnel and, raising his lamp to see more clearly, he looked around.

At once he saw Sheinna at the far end of the cave and ran towards her.

She was lying on the ground.

A rope pulled tight around her breasts bound her arms behind her back and she had a gag over her mouth.

The Duke knelt beside her.

He could see her eyes above the gag, which was only a rough tie, looking at him pleadingly.

"It is all right, my darling," he soothed her. "You are safe and no one will ever hurt you again."

He pulled away the gag and then she breathed in a broken little voice,

"*You came*, you came, I prayed that you would save me."

As she was speaking the Duke looked down at her frightened face and he thought it was impossible that this could ever have happened.

Quite involuntarily his lips came down on hers.

As he kissed her gently, he knew that it was the most wonderful moment in his entire life.

He loved her as he had never loved any woman before.

When he raised his head, she whispered, although it was difficult to hear her,

"I love you, Alpin"

"I love you too, Sheinna. I think I loved you from the first moment I saw you. I knew when you were carried away that if I lost you, I had lost something more precious than anything I have ever known."

He saw her eyes light up and he suggested gently,

"Let me release you. How could those devils treat you in such an appalling way?"

It was easy to untie the ropes because the men had not expected anyone to find her.

He could not help thinking that if, as undoubtedly Sir Ewen had intended, they had blocked up the entrance, he would never, nor would anyone else, have thought of looking for her there.

When he pulled the ropes from across her chest and round her arms, he kissed her again.

"Do you think you can walk, Sheinna?" he asked.

"I will try, but when I kicked and fought them as they were carrying me away, I hurt one of them and they hit my legs with a heavy stick."

"This will never happen to you again, my darling," the Duke promised.

"I have been praying and praying that you would save me. I think it is a miracle that God sent you."

"It is indeed an incredible miracle and one I am eternally grateful for. I could sense your distress and I could hear you calling me."

He pulled Sheinna very gently to her feet.

Then, as if he could not help himself, he placed his arms round her and kissed her again.

"You are mine," he sighed, "and I am prepared to fight for you, although I am afraid, my darling, it is going to be a long and bitter battle."

Then he suddenly remembered, and to be honest he had forgotten, that the Earl had fallen after Sir Ewen had fired his pistol at him.

He thought that perhaps it was not a very serious wound and although the Earl had collapsed onto the ground he doubted if he was dead or badly wounded.

However, he did not say anything to Sheinna as it would upset her.

She was leaning against him and he knew, although she did not complain, that her legs were hurting.

"If you will hold the lantern, my precious," he said, "I will carry you."

"You cannot do that," she protested.

"Are you insulting me?" he asked her with a smile. "You weigh very little and I have carried, in my time, far heavier things."

He put the lantern into her hand as he spoke and then he lifted her up into his arms.

"Now I feel safe," she sighed from her heart as she nestled herself into his strong chest.

"Don't speak too soon, Sheinna. I have to take you out of this place. Don't forget this tunnel and cave were closed, as I expect you were told, a long time ago because it was considered unsafe and unstable. In fact it was my great-grandfather who boarded it up and said it was never to be opened again."

"It was clever if them to put me here," Sheinna said breathlessly. "Sir Ewen kept saying, 'if I cannot have you, then no one else shall'. I think he has gone a little mad. That is how he sounded to me."

"He is not only mad but an attempted murderer and the sooner he goes to prison the better!"

Sheinna did not answer him.

The Duke carried her across the cave and they entered the tunnel that would lead them from the hiding-place.

It was then, as the Duke was moving very slowly, that Sheinna suddenly cried,

"Look, there is something shining there. I wonder if it is anything worth taking back with us."

The Duke put her down carefully and, taking the lantern from her, he held it up over his head.

Now he could see, as Sheinna had said, something was sticking out from the wall of the tunnel and shining in the light of the lantern.

The sandy soil had clearly fallen away and a little further down from the roof he could see something else shining.

The Duke thought perhaps it was a piece of tin or some implement that had been left by ancient workmen.

Thinking that it would please Sheinna to have a souvenir of this peculiar and most unexpected adventure, he put up his hand to draw out the gleaming object.

When he pulled it down, it was to his surprise *a gold goblet*.

It looked old and very discoloured and as he turned it over, he saw that there were jewels ornamenting the rim of the goblet and at the base.

Sheinna gave a little cry.

"It's a drinking cup – and a very very old one. Oh, Alpin, we have found *treasure*!"

The Duke smiled at her.

"Treasure?" he questioned.

He turned back and felt round the place from which he had pulled the cup.

Then, hardly able to believe it, he drew out another gold cup.

Behind it was a plate, also of gold, and ornamented with dozens of what were undoubtedly precious stones.

Even as Sheinna was looking at it, he put it back again in the soil and then squeezed the two cups in with it.

"Why are you doing that?" she asked. "They are yours because they are on your land."

"They are mine," he agreed, "but I think, although I may be mistaken, that you, my darling, have discovered for me the famous treasure we always believed the Vikings had taken away from my family in their ships."

Sheinna's eyes widened.

"You really think it is here?" she asked him.

"I think it has been here all the time. Perhaps the Vikings could not get it to their ships and decided to come back later and take their ill-gotten gains away with them. In the meantime they hid it under the sand in the nearest uninhabited moorland near to where they had landed."

"Oh, Alpin, what a wonderful idea! Of course I had heard about the treasure your family lost and how upset they were, but everyone always assumed that the Vikings had taken it home with them."

"We all thought so, Sheinna, but you have brought me the luck I never expected. However, the treasure must be very carefully removed in case the whole place falls in and buries it for ever. After all these years we don't want to find it only to have it all torn from us again."

"It is so exciting and it will be difficult for you not to tell your mother. She will be really thrilled, I am sure."

The Duke felt that was true and at least some of the anxiety about the upkeep of the Castle and the estate would be taken off his shoulders.

"Come along, my darling," he said. "Now we must go back and face the music – or rather your father. I think he will be feeling rather sorry for himself after Sir Ewen took a potshot at him when he came out of the tunnel."

"How dare he shoot at Papa. He is a horrid wicked man and I was quite right when I vowed that I would rather die than marry him."

'I am not going to let you marry anyone but *me,*' the Duke wanted to say.

However, at that moment they could see light at the end of the tunnel and the faces of his men were peeping in.

It was Rory who reached them first.

"You found her Ladyship, Your Grace!" he cried gleefully.

"Yes, Rory, I have and now I want to take her back to the Castle as quickly as possible."

"You be quite right, Your Grace, because there be trouble outside."

They had reached the end of the tunnel, but were still standing just inside it.

"What has happened, Rory?" the Duke asked.

"I think Sir Ewen be dead, Your Grace."

"Dead!" the Duke exclaimed. "I saw him fall, but I cannot believe that such a blow could have killed him."

"He be unconscious when they takes him away to the doctor," added Rory.

"What about my father?" Sheinna asked anxiously.

"I don't think the bullet hit him very hard," the Duke said quickly.

"It just grazed his scalp," Rory explained, "and after that he were conscious, but didn't seem to make any sense."

"So he too has gone to the doctor?"

"Yes, Your Grace, they were taken in the carriage together, and all that's left now be the MacFallin Clansmen and of course our own."

"I will go and speak to them, but first I will carry her Ladyship to our carriage."

"I thought as that's what you'd want, Your Grace, and I puts it just outside the opening of the tunnel, it's only a step or two to reach it."

"You think of everything, Rory."

He handed Rory the lantern, then picked Sheinna up in his arms.

"Now, my darling one, I am going to send you back to the Castle and you are to go straight to bed and rest."

"But I want to stay with you," murmured Sheinna.

"I want that too, but this is a great opportunity to talk to the MacFallins which I may never have again."

"Yes, of course you are right, Alpin, and I will wait for you."

"You must promise me you will," the Duke insisted firmly.

"I promise," she replied.

She looked into his eyes as she spoke and he knew that she wanted him to kiss her.

"I love you, Sheinna" he whispered tenderly.

Then, as they reached the carriage, he lifted her very gently into it.

"Take her home, Rory, and I expect there will be some other conveyance for me."

"Quite a lot of our men've joined us, Your Grace, and they'll want to hear what be said. Then they'll escort Your Grace safely back to the Castle."

"I am sure they will, Rory."

He noticed that there was another of his carriages just inside the field.

Then he walked over to where the MacFallins were gathered in a large group and they were obviously waiting for him.

They must have remained after the Earl had been taken off to the doctor and were waiting to see if the Duke had rescued Lady Sheinna or if she had been lost inside the Vikings hiding-place.

As he walked towards them, he saw that some of them were sitting down on the ground and his own men were talking to them in quite a friendly fashion.

There was nothing, he mused, like a tragedy or an unexpected excitement to bring men together.

As he reached them, they made a move as if to get up and he put up his hand.

"Stay where you are," he called out, "I want to talk to you and this is an opportunity I don't want to lose."

CHAPTER SEVEN

Sheinna was dreaming that the Duke was kissing her.

Then suddenly she felt that he was!

She looked up and he was saying,

"You look so very lovely when you are asleep, my darling."

"Where have you been? What has happened?" she asked a little breathlessly.

"I have so much to tell you, Sheinna. I should not be in your room, but I could not wait."

"Tell me, please tell me," she begged.

She pulled herself up a little further on her pillows.

The Duke was gazing at her with such love in his eyes that she felt her heart turn a somersault.

"Please tell me, Alpin, what you did after you sent me back to the Castle."

"I went to talk to the Clansmen and to my surprise they listened attentively to me and then the elders of your father's Clan *actually* agreed with me!"

"Oh, how wonderful," Sheinna exclaimed.

"I was very thrilled. The leader of the elders, who is indeed an intelligent man, said he believed I was right that hostilities had gone too far and for too long. It was time we thought of Scotland rather than the feud between our own Clans."

"That is exactly what you have said, Alpin."

"They then told me that the one change they would enjoy more than anything and which would unite the two Clans would be our marriage."

Sheinna drew in her breath.

"You really mean I can marry you, Alpin?"

"I have every intention of marrying you even if everyone in the world was against it," replied the Duke. "But it makes it far easier if the Clans willingly unite as we are uniting and we can therefore start afresh without this endless disagreeableness between our peoples."

"It will be wonderful," Sheinna sighed. "I want to love your Clansmen as well as mine."

"All you have to do," the Duke said very softly, "is to love me."

"I *do* love you, Alpin. I love you more than I can possibly say. But please you must go on telling me what else has happened."

"It's very difficult for me when I want to kiss you, but I think you should know and I hope it does not upset you too much, that your father is unlikely to recover from the pistol-shot wound."

Sheinna drew in her breath.

"Is it as bad – as that?" she asked hesitantly.

"He is alive and the doctors think he will live for perhaps a year or more. But his brain will undoubtedly be affected."

"Oh, poor Papa! Even though I do find him very difficult and to be truthful, I cannot love him, but I don't want him to suffer."

"I don't think he will suffer. He has what they call a brain haemorrhage and the world will seem indistinct to him, but we will see he is comfortable and has two nurses to look after him, which on my instructions the doctor has now organised."

"Then I must not worry too much."

"That is what I was thinking about when I arranged it," the Duke told her.

"And – Sir Ewen?"

"He had a stroke when he was hit on the back of the head. He is unconscious and the doctors expect him to die at any moment. Although it may sound unkind, I don't think that anyone will grieve for him. They assured me that, as he is unconscious, he is not in any pain."

Sheinna closed her eyes for a moment and the Duke knew that she was thinking there was no possibility now of her being forced into marriage with Sir Ewen.

"It's *me* you are going to marry," he asserted.

"You are reading my thoughts – "

"Just as you read mine," he answered. "And if you read them at this very moment, you will know how much I love you."

Sheinna made a sound of happiness.

"Oh, Alpin. It is so wonderful that we have found each other. We both wanted to marry for love and that is just what we are doing."

"Exactly," he agreed, "but you have forgotten to ask me a very important question."

"What is that?" she quizzed him.

"About the Viking treasure we found. On my way back from the doctors I went into the tunnel again. I still can hardly believe it, but I now think that all the treasure stolen from the Castle by the Vikings is there."

"How is that possible?"

"I think now that it may have been hidden there by the Viking marauders themselves when they found out that the people hid from them in the tunnel or else, and this is I think the most likely story, some of the most loyal of our Clan realised that the Vikings were rifling the Castle and ambushed them on their return to their boat. They either killed and buried them or allowed them to escape without the treasure they had stolen from my family."

Sheinna was listening wide-eyed and then the Duke went on,

"When the Vikings sailed away, the Clansmen took the treasure, I should think at night, and hid it in the tunnel. It would have been far too dangerous to tell anyone it was there. They therefore kept silent and the secret died with them."

Sheinna gave a little cry.

"You could write a novel about it. It is the most exciting tale I have ever heard. Do you think everything is there that was taken from the Castle?"

"I have been careful not to disturb it too much, but it seems that there is a good chance that all the treasure is there in the tunnel waiting for us."

"How wonderful, Alpin, and I am sure that it was my prayers which led you to find me and now you will be able to restore the Castle as you have always wanted."

"I shall hate to sell any of the treasure, but it's more important that the Castle should be restored and the houses of our people renovated. As your father rightly pointed out to me, we also require many more river watchers."

"Perhaps there will be no need for you to sell all the treasure," said Sheinna, "because you can use my money."

"*Your money?*" the Duke echoed and before she could reply, he added, "but, darling, I am afraid we need not hundreds of pounds but many thousands."

"My grandmother was very rich and although it did annoy Papa, she left me everything she possessed when she died. But I am not allowed to touch the money until I am either twenty-one or married."

The Duke was so astonished that for the moment he was silent.

"Are you telling me that you are an heiress?"

"I don't know whether I can compete with Mary-Lee, but I think Grandmama left me nearly seven hundred thousand pounds. Of course I am only too happy that you should spend it on making our home as beautiful as you wish it to be and on whatever the estate may require."

The Duke put his hand up to his forehead.

"I am dreaming," he cried. "I know I am dreaming. This cannot be true! We will wake up to find you have to marry Sir Ewen and I have to marry Mary-Lee!"

Sheinna laughed.

"That was just a nasty nightmare. The truth is, you have won yet another battle although you were not aware of it."

"I do believe, Sheinna, that God sent you especially down from Heaven to help me. I have been looking for you all my life. When that swine carried you away, I was frantic. I was terrified, when I heard he had turned down the coast road, that he intended to take you out to sea and it might be impossible to ever find you again."

"But you *did* find me, Alpin. I was praying all the time I was in the carriage with him and when those horrible men bound me up and dragged me into the Viking hiding-place."

"I sensed that you were calling me and it made me even more afraid that you might be putting out to sea and I would have to search every ocean, which I would have done, to find you again."

He knew that he had been very conscious of her calling for him and it was a feeling he could hardly believe was true until he had spied Sir Ewen's carriage outside the entrance to the tunnel.

And if it had not been there he knew he would have gone straight on into the village and he would have been quite certain they had put out to sea.

"I will never doubt again," he said, "the importance or the value of prayer. I have found you, my darling, and now I will never lose you – *never*, never!"

"That is what I want you to tell me, because I love you with all my heart. If we had to live in a cottage rather than in this glorious Castle, I would still be happy because I was with you."

The Duke then kissed Sheinna until they were both breathless.

Eventually he raised hid head and declared,

"I have to go and talk to my own elders about our wedding. I told Rory to bring them here, for they must not feel they are being left out of the arrangements."

"Of course not, Alpin, I will get up and be waiting for you downstairs when you have finished with them."

"Promise me, Sheinna, you will not disappear or be kidnapped again."

He was teasing, but Sheinna gave a little shiver.

"I have never been so frightened in my entire life and I thought I would never see you again."

"But now you will see me for always and for ever – and I will grudge every moment we are not together."

He kissed her again and walked towards the door.

Sheinna looked round at the clock and saw to her astonishment that it was already approaching dinnertime.

She had been so totally exhausted after the terrible experience of being manhandled by Sir Ewen's men that she had fallen into a deep sleep.

It was just as men did on battlefields after fighting a battle. They would fall sleep into a deep unconsciousnesss that would often alarm those who had come to search for them.

Sheinna rang the bell and the maids brought in her bath and then helped her to dress in her most glamorous gown.

She hoped that after all this commotion she might be dining alone with the Duke.

Suddenly she realised that she had not asked him whether his mother was distressed by all the happenings of the day.

But the maid told her,

"We didn't disturb Her Grace by tellin' her what be happenin' till luncheon time when she questioned me why you, my Lady, and His Grace wasn't there."

"I do hope she was not worried too much about us."

"She be a little distressed until you returned. Then she hears from Mr. Rory that His Grace had gone to the village."

Sheinna did not ask any further questions, but went down to the drawing room.

There was no one present and then instinctively she walked to the window to look out at the sea.

The sun was just sinking behind the moors and she could not imagine a more stunning view anywhere in the world.

Then the door of the drawing room opened and the Duke entered and because they were alone she ran towards him and put her arms round his neck.

"Is everything all right, Alpin?" she asked.

He kissed her.

Then still holding her very closely against him, he replied,

"Everything, my darling, is even better than I could have expected. Everyone wants to help make our wedding the most exciting celebration that has occurred at the Castle for at least two hundred years!"

Sheinna laughed and as he had spoken so seriously he laughed at himself.

*

Their wedding day was arranged to take place in two weeks time.

Although the Duke did not wish to upset Sheinna, he hurried the arrangements as he was worried that the doctors had said that her father might die, in which case she would be in deep mourning for many months.

The Earl, however, was in most capable hands and the nurses assured the Duke that he was living in a world of his own and reasonably happy.

He was blissfully unaware of what was happening to his daughter, his family or his Clan.

The Duke tried to contact Sheinna's elder brother, Bruce, who she had not seen for some years. He had been abroad taking part in the Crimean War and was now in Africa.

There was no chance, he was told, of his being able to be back in time for the wedding.

The Duke expected, although he did not say so, that Bruce would resign from the Army and come back to look after his Clan, but all this would take time and he had no intention of waiting.

"I have arranged," he told Sheinna, "that you will be given away by the most senior of the MacFallin elders, who has known you ever since you were a baby and I have found him to be a charming man."

"Oh, I like him too and he has always been very kind to me, but living with my Grandmama I have not seen him for years."

"He is looking forward to seeing you and as he is very tall and good-looking, although he is over seventy, he will certainly make a very picturesque appearance at our wedding."

He most tactfully had arranged for it to take place in the Kirk on the estate belonging to the Earl and it was, as it happened, much larger than the Kirk near the Castle and all the MacFallin Clan were delighted that the wedding would be celebrated on MacFallin ground.

The wedding breakfast, however, was to be held at the Castle and the pipers of both Clans were to escort the married couple from one place to the other.

In fact as the day grew nearer, Sheinna learnt that members of both Clans were determined to make it, as the Duke had suggested, a great festive ceremony.

It would celebrate not only their marriage but the union of the Clans.

The only person who did not agree that this was a marvellous idea was naturally the Countess of Dunkeld.

She was still upsetting the Dowager Duchess with her criticisms and complaints and discouraging many of the McBarens from celebrating the marriage.

The Duke felt that he must speak to her husband – an intelligent man who had no wish to quarrel with anyone.

He had not listened to his wife's moaning about the MacFallins, but he had only occasionally managed to make her see that she was being far too over-dramatic and over-aggressive about them.

When the Duke appealed to the Earl of Dunkeld for support, he most sensibly took his wife, his daughter and Mary-Lee away on a tour of the Orkney Islands.

He knew that the fishing would be excellent and the people there were always most hospitable.

No one regretted that the Countess would not be present at the marriage ceremony.

*

Everyone else grew more and more enthusiastic as the day drew nearer.

The Duke and Sheinna had so many arrangements to make that there was hardly time to worry about anything else.

It was with great difficulty that Sheinna managed to obtain a delightful wedding dress from Edinburgh.

The Dowager Duchess produced the lace veil that had been in the family for generations and she insisted that Sheinna should wear the majestic ancestral tiara she had worn herself at her own wedding.

"It has stayed in the safe ever since," she confided, "because it is too big and too flamboyant for me to wear, unless I was invited to Windsor Castle!"

"You are quite certain you don't mind me having it?" Sheinna asked. "I know it will please Alpin if I wear it and the one my grandmother left me is not so magnificent nor, I must point out, so heavy!"

The Dowager Duchess laughed.

"I am afraid mine is rather heavy, but you need not have it on for too long, unless you stay very late at your wedding feast, which I am sure Alpin will not wish to do."

She realised that the Dowager Duchess was teasing her, but she had to admit that the tiara was fantastic and finer than anything anyone locally had ever seen.

Rory had cleaned it until it shone almost like a star in the sky and with her own family's jewellery Sheinna felt that she would glitter as every member of the Clan wished.

Early in the morning on her wedding day Sheinna jumped out of bed and looked out of the window to see if the sun was shining.

She had left the Castle the day before to sleep in her own home and, although she hated to admit it, it looked extremely dull and gloomy after staying in the Castle.

"I hate you having to leave, even for one night," the Duke protested. "I am so afraid you will disappear and I will have to spend the rest of my life searching for you."

"I will never do that, darling Alpin, but it is only correct that I should stay in my own home before I come to yours."

"You promise me you will be in the Kirk tomorrow morning – and I will not wake up to find that I have lost you again?"

"I promise I will be there," answered Sheinna. "I know it will be such a wonderful day not only for us but for your people and mine, who are uniting for the first time in more than four hundred years."

"How could they have been so stupid? How could our ancestors have spent so much time fostering the feud instead of trying to stop it?"

"Which is what you have now achieved and it is wonderful of you," said Sheinna. "I am certain that before you die, you will be declared a Saint!"

The Duke held up his hands.

"I have no wish to be a Saint. I just want to be your loving husband and to take you to so many places in the world which neither of us have seen and which will give us new ideas and new inpiration."

He paused for a moment before he added,

"I am so delighted that your brother, who you tell me is not in the least like your father in his hatred of the

McBarens, is giving up his Army Commission and coming back to run the estate."

"That is just what he says he will do as quickly as he can, but he told me in his letter it will take time for him to quit the Army. In the meantime we must leave it to the elders to look after the Clan, as I am sure they will do."

"Some of them are delightful. I have always been very fond of my own elders and I cannot help feeling, now they have met, they will enjoy each other's company."

"Of course they will and you must help them with new ideas and perhaps a certain amount of money even though we want a great deal of it for ourselves."

"If we all work together, there will be no further problems. It is what, my beautiful one, you and I will plan together."

"You are wonderful, Alpin, and I do love you."

He gave her a long, passionate and fervent kiss before reluctantly he left her and went back to the Castle.

"I will be counting every moment until you are with me again," he sighed before he left.

"I will be praying that tomorrow comes quickly."

The house was packed with her relations, many of whom she had never even seen before. They had quarrelled with her father, but now they knew he was no longer there, they had eagerly accepted their invitations to the wedding.

She had also asked several of her closest friends in London and those who had loved her grandmother and in fact the house was full and some had to share a room.

Much the same was happening at the Castle.

When the Duke started to send out his invitations, he had no idea that he had so many relatives or indeed so many friends.

He was very touched by the way so many of them were prepared to come all the way to Scotland to attend his wedding.

It was a very acceptable wedding gift when the Earl of Dunkeld told him that, as he would be in the Orkneys with his family, his house was at the Duke's disposal.

The Duke was extremely grateful to him and even more grateful that the Countess would not be present to try to spoil his wedding day.

"Everything," he said to his mother that evening, "has gone exactly as I want it to go. I know you now think Sheinna is the right wife for me."

"I think she is absolutely charming," the Dowager Duchess said. "I know, dearest boy, how much she loves you and that is what I am really happy about.

"I was always afraid you would be married for your title, but I know that Sheinna would marry you if you were just an ordinary Clansman and without this beautiful Castle which will be a real home for you both."

"I know, Mama, and I was desperately afraid of being married for anything but myself. I thought perhaps I would never marry anyone."

"That would have been disastrous. Now, my dear Alpin, as you know, I am looking forward eagerly to my grandchildren!"

The Duke kissed her cheek.

"You are going far too fast, Mama. Let's get our wedding over first before you begin to plan which rooms will be the nurseries."

"Of course you will have the rooms you had when you were a boy!"

The Duke laughed because he was only teasing her.

*

He was as thrilled as Sheinna when he saw that the sun was shining.

He rose early to supervise the roasting of the stag, which was to take place in the grounds of the Castle and there was plenty of food and whisky for the Clansmen.

For his personal guests a special luncheon had been arranged in the garden. It would have been disastrous if it was raining and they had to carry everything back indoors.

It was Sheinna's idea that they should eat amongst the flowers.

A local orchestra was to play soft romantic music, except of course when the speeches were being made by himself and other members of both families.

When Sheinna was fnally dressed and came down the stairs of her own home, those present thought that no bride could look more enchanting or happier.

She had chosen several small bridesmaids, none of them over fifteen, from her own relatives and some of the Duke's.

They were dressed in white and carried bouquets of roses and white heather and there were two small boys aged seven to carry her train.

When she stepped out of the carriage at the door of the Kirk, the crowd outside cheered and clapped her, not just because she looked so beautiful, but because they too were excited and thrilled by such a magnificent wedding.

Not all the guests could be seated inside the Kirk and a great number had to remain outside.

When she walked slowly up the aisle on the arm of the senior elder, she saw the Duke standing waiting for her and thought no one could be luckier or happier than she.

The Marriage Service was short, but spoken with a deep sincerity by the Minister, who had actually baptised Sheinna after she was born.

When they knelt for the Blessing, she felt sure that God had protected and looked after them both through so many dangers.

It was entirely due to Him that on this special day the Clans were forgetting all the past rancour and bitterness between them. In the future they would be friendly and work together for the good of Scotland.

The Duke had said much the same in the speech he had made at the wedding breakfast.

When they applauded him because, a little to their surprise, he had spoken so eloquently, more than one of his relatives declared,

"You will have to spend some time in the future speaking for Scotland in the House of Lords, Alpin. We are so desperately short of young men like you who really care for Scotland and our future well-being."

"I will do everything I can," the Duke promised.

Sheinna knew they were delighted with him and they were quite right in realising he had a way of speaking which made people not only listen but agree with him.

The pipers were still playing when, having changed their wedding clothes, the bride and bridegroom, now the Duke and Duchess of Barenlock, left the Castle by walking through the garden and down to the jetty where the Duke's yacht was waiting for them.

It was decorated with flags and endless flowers and when she saw it, Sheinna gave a cry of delight.

"I did not think a yacht could look so beautiful," she sighed.

"Everything has to be beautiful for you," the Duke said, "because you are the most beautiful girl in the whole wide world!"

They smiled at each other before stepping aboard to receive the congratulations of the Captain and the crew.

When the yacht finally started to move away down the bay, the music of the pipes was heard long after the cheers and cries of 'good luck and good fortune' no longer reached them.

When at last they were well out to sea, the Duke suggested,

"Let's go below. I so want to kiss you, my darling Sheinna, and tell you how much I love you, again and again and again."

She smiled at him.

"That is what I want too, but there is plenty of time and I think for a few moments we must watch while we move away from Scotland and into a new world which we have made ours today. A world where there is only love and happiness."

The Duke placed his arm round her and they stood gazing at the moors fading into the distance and had their last glimpse of the Castle.

Then she went below and found as she expected that the Master cabin, which was now hers, was decorated with white flowers and white heather.

"It's so fantastic!" she exclaimed.

Closing the door behind him, the Duke sighed,

"And you are so fantastic too."

He took the wreath from her head and then he was kissing her wildly and passionately.

"I love you. I love you," he cried. "I cannot tell you how much until we have had dinner which the chef has specially prepared for us. Of course we will have to ask the Captain and the other Officers to drink our health."

"I will join you in the Saloon in two minutes," Sheinna promised.

Reluctantly he took his arms from around her.

"You are so magnificent that I want to shut you up in a cage so no one can go near you or see you except me!"

"If you do that, Alpin, you will be bored with me in a week!"

"I could never be bored with you, my darling one, in a thousand years."

Because the dinner was so good and they had to thank the chef for it and then open their wedding presents that very touchingly the Captain and crew had given them, it was dark when they finally went below.

They had already sailed quite a long way South and the yacht stopped in a quiet bay and anchored there for the night.

The only hint to tell Sheinna that she was still at sea was the soft lap of the waves against the side of the yacht.

She was in bed with her fair hair falling over her shoulders when the Duke came into the Master cabin.

He was wearing a long dark rather military-looking robe.

For a moment he just sat down on the side of the bed and gazed at her.

"This is the second time, my darling, I have seen you in bed. Each time you look lovelier than you did before. I was thinking today when we were married that no man had ever had a more beautiful bride."

"I want to look beautiful for you, Alpin, but you forget how handsome you are yourself in your family kilt and your special ancestral sporran."

The Duke's eyes twinkled.

"I can see I have a great deal to tell you about myself and it is something I will definitely enjoy."

"So will I," Sheinna enthused.

"And I will want to know everything about you," he said. "But first I have to tell you how much I love you."

"He took off his robe, slid into bed and pulled her close to him.

He felt the softness of her body melting into his and knew the love which consumed them both was making her tremble.

He could only thank God for all he had received today by making, if at all possible, others as happy as he and Sheinna were.

Then his arms tightened round her and he drew her closer and still closer to him.

"I just love and adore you," he sighed. "The most thrilling moment of my life will be when I teach you all about love."

"If I am ignorant in my mind about love, my heart is beating for you, Alpin, and I have never known such a wonderful feeling as the one which is now moving within my body."

The Duke knew she was trying to put into words what was almost inexpressible.

Then he kissed her and went on kissing her until finally when he made her his, he knew that they had fought a strange and unusual battle to win each other.

But they had won.

Now their happiness would affect both their Clans, and the men and women in them would all benefit because they themselves were so happy.

"I adore you," the Duke repeated. "But there are no words for me to tell you how much."

"I love and worship you, my adorable husband. I love you with my heart, my mind and my body – they are all yours, Alpin."

As the Duke felt the wonder of his love moving deeply within him, he knew that they touched the stars in Heaven.

They had received the Blessing of God because love comes from God, is part of God, and is always there for those who seek it.

As the waves lapped softly against the sides of the yacht, Sheinna whispered,

"I love you, oh my darling, wonderful Alpin, I love you, I adore you."

"And I love you, Sheinna. You are mine, not only for now but for all Eternity.

And the yacht sailed on into the glorious Heaven that awaited them over the horizon.